# King of New York 4

Lock Down Publications and Ca$h
Presents

# KING OF NEW YORK 4
## A Novel by *T.J. EDWARDS*

# Lock Down Publications
P.O. Box 870494
Mesquite, Tx 75187

**Visit our website @**
www.lockdownpublications.com

**Lock Down Publications**
**Like our page on Facebook: Lock Down Publications @**
www.facebook.com/lockdownpublications.ldp
Cover design and layout by: **Dynasty Cover Me**
Book interior design by: **Shawn Walker**
Edited by: **Tisha Andrews**

# Stay Connected with Us!

Text **LOCKDOWN** to 22828 to stay up-to-date with new releases, sneak peaks, contests and more...

Thank you.

# Submission Guideline.

Submit the first three chapters of your completed manuscript to ldpsubmissions@gmail.com, subject line: Your book's title. The manuscript must be in a .doc file and sent as an attachment. Document should be in Times New Roman, double spaced and in size 12 font. Also, provide your synopsis and full contact information. If sending multiple submissions, they must each be in a separate email.

Have a story but no way to send it electronically? You can still submit to LDP/Ca$h Presents. Send in the first three chapters, written or typed, of your completed manuscript to:

LDP: Submissions Dept
Po Box 870494
Mesquite, Tx 75187

*DO NOT send original manuscript. Must be a duplicate.*

Provide your synopsis and a cover letter containing your full contact information.

Thanks for considering LDP and Ca$h Presents.

T.J. Edwards

# Chapter 1

## Showbiz

The constant tick, tick, tick sound of the jump rope skipping across the pavement sounded in my ears as the little girls double dutched on the playground behind me. The bouncing of a basketball along with the smack talking of the two teenage boys that were playing each other one on one in a battle for supremacy. The sun beamed in my face, causing me to squint my eyes. Sweat slid down my forehead and dripped off of my chin. A slight breeze from the wind offered a small chance of relief from the hot spring day in New York City.

I made my way across the small parking lot with my heart thumping in my chest. My .45 was tucked safely in my waistband loaded with ten hollow points. I had visions of using every bullet. I closed the distance between myself and Flex with nothing but anger and frustration on my mind.

It had been more than three months prior that I fronted Flex three kilos of heroin. He gave me his word that once he popped the dope, he'd give me fifty a piece for each kilo, which was a hundred and fifty thousand dollars. The dope was more than ninety percent and in the city of New York, to find any type of product that was more than seventy percent was a steal. I could have easily charged him sixty thousand a piece and never fronted him in the first place. But you see, Flex and I had history.

Back when we were in high school and I'd just stepped off of the stoop, we'd lay niggas on their stomachs and put gats in their mouths until we emptied their safes, taking anything of value we wanted. He also stood beside me and bust his gun on numerous occasions. Even though he was a Brooklyn nigga and I was from Harlem, somehow we managed to get along. In the city of New York, that was unheard of. Most niggas stayed in their own boroughs, repping their own hoods. But one summer, I served three months in juvenile hall. Flex and I had met up on the inside and just clicked. That's before we found out where each other was from.

After that revelation, we found out that we had a lot in common and had even fucked some of the same hoes. After we got out, we started hitting licks together. Over time, we lost contact because of the life we lived individually. Then a little over three months, he'd rolled up on me. We had kicked it for a few hours when he had asked me for a favor. He needed help getting back on his feet. Even though I hadn't seen him in a while, it was hard for me to forget how he'd always stood by me when we were kids, bussing niggas down.

I had five kilos of my family's heroin in my truck at the time and against my better judgment, I wound up giving him, or should I say, "fronted" him three kilos. After that day, I hadn't heard from him since.

I didn't give a fuck how cool we were, I wasn't the type of nigga to play about my money. I was Juanito Vega but known to the streets as Showbiz. A living muthafucking legend and I was getting ready to put my stamp all on this nigga's ass.

Flex, a dark-skinned nigga with long dreadlocks, saw me coming across the parking lot and jumped to his feet. He dropped the bottle of Armor All he'd been holding, while buffing the rims on his Cadillac Escalade.

Flex's eyes bucked. "Yo, Showbiz. Look, I know I ain't got up wit' you, but I just been on some other shit. I should have that bread for you in a few weeks. I mean you know how it is out here."

I shook my head. "N'all, fuck nigga. It's been more than three months already. You gon' give me my shit right now." I upped my .45 and smacked him across the face with it, splitting his shit. He fell to one knee and held his face.

He looked down at the blood on his fingers. "Fuck, man! Shoot this bitch ass nigga. What the fuck y'all waiting on?" Flex hollered.

Two of the niggas standing outside of the trucks with him, opened the doors to the Escalade and reached inside of them. I saw one of them come up with a nickel-plated Mach. He cocked it and slammed the door that blocked his view of me, before leveling his weapon and aiming it in my direction.

My eyes got as big as paper plates. I aimed at him and pulled the trigger.

*Boom! Boom! Boom!*

The bullets flew out of my .45 and slammed into his chest, filling it with big bloody holes. He threw his arms into the air before falling backwards and dropping the Mach. Before I could turn around to break away from them, Flex stood up and aimed at me.

*Bocka! Bocka! Bocka! Bocka!*

His bullets punched into my torso and threw me backwards on the pavement. The stinging in my torso told me that at least one of them had penetrated my bulletproof vest. It felt like a flaming nail was burning me. I placed my hand on my chest and struggled to get up as I heard more shots rang out along with the screaming from the little girls on the playground.

"Get down!" someone yelled.

*Boom! Boom! Boom! Boom!*

I saw sparks fly from the Escalade in front of me. Flex ducked behind one of them before bussing toward the playground.

*Bocka! Bocka! Bocka!*

I slowly got to my feet and took off running toward my car. I looked up toward the basketball courts and saw my little brother, Tristian, bussing his gun at Flex and his crew. Then he took off running, diving on top of one of the little girls that was at the park as more gunfire came in my direction. Bullets slammed into my Porsche. I ran and jump into it, then over it. I stood up and fired three shots in Flex's direction.

*Boom! Boom! Boom!*

My son, Maine, sat in the back seat of my Porsche with his hands over his ears. "Ahh! Ahh! Help! Ahh!" he hollered.

I peeked over the side of the Porsche as one of Flex's men with a Tech .9 in his hands began to spray my whip. Then he sprayed the playground where Tristian was bussing. He ran in their direction, unloading his clip. I aimed and tried to squeeze my trigger, but it wouldn't budge. I squeezed it as hard as I could but nothing happened. "Fuck, why this shit gotta happen right now?" I begin to panic.

"Daddy! Daddy! Help me! Help me!" Maine hollered, reaching out for me.

*Bocka! Bocka! Bocka!*

Flex's bullets rocked the side of my drop top Porsche. "It's Brooklyn, nigga! You should of never came over here, Showbiz! Now yo' bitch ass is about to die! You and your son!" he hollered.

He stood up and got to bucking at my ride again, making it jerk from side to side. I ducked down and bit into my bottom lip. I didn't know what to do. I'd given my brother, Tristian, my last gun out of the glove box. I was stuck. I had to get my son out of the line of fire. It was the least I could do as the sun seemed to become a million degrees hotter.

I opened the passenger's door and pulled Maine out of the Porsche beside me. He was crying his little eyes out. Flex reached into his Escalade and came out with a Mach .90. He ran into the middle of the parking lot and got to spitting at my ride bullet after bullet. I could hear the bullets tanking into the paint job.

"Aww, you must be out of bullets, son. Oh, that's yo' ass, Money!" He ran back to his truck. "Come on, son. Let's finish his bitch ass," Flex ordered his shooter.

The gunmen holding the tech ran and jumped into the truck along side of Flex. Their Escalade backed out, crashing into my Porsche. I peeked over the top of my whip and saw Flex's window roll down. He stuck his arm out of it along with the Mach .90. Before he could start shooting, I jumped up and took off running. There was a big dumpster about fifty feet away. I knew if I made it to it, I could shield myself from his barrage of bullets.

So that's where I was headed. It didn't dawn on my me until I got half way there that my six-year old son was with me who probably needed me to carry him to safety, as well. But when it clicked, I stopped in my tracks and turned around. "Maine! Aww, shit!" I took off running toward him.

The sun seemed to shine directly into my eyes. All of the wind felt as if it stopped. There was a low pitch hum in my ears. My heart pounded louder than it ever had before. I felt like I could feel it in my throat. A big smile spread across Flex's face as soon as Maine jumped up to run to me. He bit his bottom lip and aimed.

*Bocka! Bocka! Bocka! Bocka!*

I watched the bullets spit out of the barrel of his Mach as if it were in slow motion. The first series entered into the side of Maine's head and knocked massive chunks out of it. They spun him around before he fell on his back. The second series filled his torso with holes before the third series sprayed along the concrete, missing him entirely.

I continued to run toward him. Flex's truck sped away, it's back bumper scraping against the pavement after they sped out of the parking lot and hopped the curb. I ran over and fell beside Maine.

"Son! Son! Aww, shit!" I picked him up into my arms and looked down at him, feeling my heart tear into two. His face was half gone. His brains leaked out of the opening Flex's bullets had caused.

He felt lighter than usual. There was a constant gurgling sound coming from the holes in his midsection. It was enough to make any man go crazy. I felt the tears sliding down my cheeks. My heart was hurting. I felt like a victim. I felt betrayed. I knew I had let my son down, that because of me, he had been killed.

Had I never approached Flex with him in the car, he would have still been alive. What kind of a father failed their child the way I just had? I felt lower than scum. I broke into a fit of tears, holding my baby. He'd lost his life only a few weeks after his sixth birthday and it had been all my fault. I slowly laid him down on the pavement and closed his eyes.

I looked toward the playground and saw Tristian was still laid out on his stomach. Him and the little girl that he'd jumped on top of for whatever reason. I could smell the gunpowder in the air and hear the sirens in the distance, causing me to panic. I jumped up and ran over to my brother. "Tristian! Tristian, get up, man! The police on their way!" I hollered.

He moved slowly and looked up at me. "I'm hit, Showbiz. Them bitch niggas hit me," he groaned. "And she is, too." He looked down at the little girl that was in his arms. Her eyes were closed. She whimpered and took deep breaths. Blood oozed out of the holes in her lower back.

I didn't give a fuck about her. I didn't even know whose kid she was. My son was dead. As far as I was concerned, nothing mattered more than that. Not even my brother being wounded at that time. Her face was scrunched into a ball. I could sense she was in some serious pain.

"Bruh, Maine is dead. He's dead, Tristian. That fuck nigga shot my baby! What am I supposed to do?"

I took off running after hearing the sirens that seemed to have gotten closer. When I got back to Maine's body, I picked him up and placed him on the back seat of my Porsche. I got behind the wheel and stormed out of the parking lot.

\* \* \*

After running every red light and speeding past every car I could without crashing, it took me ten minutes to make it to my crib. I pulled up into the back alley, jumped out and put Maine into my arms, before running with him to the back door. Once there, I began to kick on it. His blood ran down my arms and dropped off my elbows. "Tori! Tori! Baby, open the door! Maine is hurt!" I hollered.

I looked down at my son as another portion of his brains dropped into the back yard. I felt sick on the stomach. Tori looked out of the back window first before running down the back steps and throwing the door open. "Oh my God! Jehovah, no! Please Father, no!" she screamed, trying to take him out of my arms. "What happened to him?"

I released him from my arms and led us into the back hallway where I closed the door and fell to my knees. "Baby, it was Flex. That bitch ass nigga from Brooklyn. He shot me up, too. See?" I showed her the holes in my shirt before pulling it over my head and unsnapping my vest. There were three bleeding punctures in my chest where the bullets had pierced the kevlar.

Tori fell to the ground with him. "No, Showbiz! Why? Why would any man want to kill a child? He was just a baby. This isn't fair!" she cried, rocking back and forth. I crawled over to her and placed my arm around her shoulders.

"He ain't gon' get away with this shit, ma. This nigga ain't gon' get away with killing my son. Everybody he loves, everybody he fuck wit', I'm killing all of 'em. I won't rest until all of them bitches are in body bags. That's on my mother!" I hollered, looking down at my son with tears running down my cheeks.

T.J. Edwards

# Chapter 2

Maine's funeral was held a week later. Instead of contacting the authorities and going through that whole process, I called up my old man and asked him how should we go about handling the whole ordeal. He assured me that it would be taken care of. I didn't ask him what that meant. All I knew is that the police never contacted me. Had I been, I still would have never opened my mouth.

In my opinion, this wasn't a matter for the police to sort out. Maine was my only child, my first-born son. There was no way I would have gotten any spiritual relief if the police had locked up Flex before I got a hold of his ass. I had plans for him and I knew I would not be able to sleep until they were brought into fruition.

I looked into my baby's casket and wiped away the tears that slid down my cheeks. I had on a pair of triple tinted Ray Ban sunglasses that offset my black on black suit. There was a black net over his face to shield the family from the sight of his injuries.

My father and I made sure his funeral was a private affair just for our closest relatives. If a person wasn't related to my son by blood, they were unable to attend. Tristian came up behind me and placed his hand on my shoulder. "Bruh, how are you holding up?" he asked.

I shook my head and continued to look my baby over. I was wishing that I had spent more time with him. I couldn't believe I had been such a terrible father relationship wise to my kid. I hated I allowed my utter disdain for his mother to affect the relationship that he and I shared. That was petty of me.

I knew that I would never forgive myself. I sighed and shrugged my shoulders. "I lost my kid, bruh. I don't know how this shit gon' effect me down the road. One thing I do know is that I'm about to bring New York to its knees over my seed, Dunn. That's my word."

I blinked and more tears fell out of my eyes. Instead of wiping them away, I just let 'em flow. I heard a bunch of murmuring behind me, then Tristian smacked his lips. "Aww, shit. Here we go with this bullshit."

"Dang, can y'all let somebody else see my nephew? Y'all been up here long enough," Ebony quipped. She bumped Tristian out of the way and tried to do the same to me.

I took my glasses off of my face and mugged her yellow ass. "Bitch, you already know I ain't the one. You can take that punk shit somewhere else. Sit yo' ass down until I'm finished up here or else."

I slid my glasses back on to my face. I ain't feel like going through that drama with Ebony's ass. Out of all of baby mother's sisters, she was the one that kept up all of the bullshit. After Punkin, Maine's mother, had passed away from complications with her pregnancy, I'd allowed Ebony to take custody of my son because I wasn't really ready to be a single father.

I was still a dope boy, running wild in the streets of New York. I couldn't see myself having some kid attached at my hip twenty-four seven. I had way too much beef and not enough patience for all of that shit. It wasn't until I started to fucking with my baby mother's sister, Tori, that I'd wanted custody of my son back. And that was only because Tori and my son had a strong bond and relationship.

Once Ebony found out that Tori and I were an item, she hurried and kicked Maine to the curb and I regained custody of him. She and I had never had strong bond or liked each other. I think it was because I'd picked Punkin over her back in the day even though back then, Ebony thought she was the shit.

She was five feet three inches tall, red boned with hazel eyes and long, natural, reddish-brown hair with a nice body to go along with every thing else. She had real big titties that looked good on her. Even though I didn't like her, I still had to keep shit real. She was bad. "You don't scare me, Showbiz. I ain't worried about you doing nothing to me. Now get the fuck out of my way so I can see my nephew and get the fuck out of here!" She rolled her eyes and tried to push me out of the way again.

I took a step to the side and grabbed her by her neck, before slapping her across the face as hard as I could.

*Wham!*

She yelped and fell to the floor. She scooted backward on her ass, holding her face that was bright red from where I'd hit her loud mouth ass. "I hate you! It's your fault that my nephew is dead! One day, somebody gon' kill yo' ass, Showbiz. Mark those words!" she screamed.

I closed the distance between us and snatched her up by her hair. The family in the pews ran to one side of the church in a frenzy. "Bitch, I'm sick of your mouth. You always got somethin' to say." I smacked her across the face again, then back handed her, dropping her ass back to the floor. She curled into a ball, crying her eyes out.

"I hate him so much. I swear to God I do."

"Get this bitch out of here before I stomp a mud hole in her ass!" I snapped at Tristian. Tori rushed to her side along with my brother and picked her up. She staggered to her feet, crying loudly.

My father, Chico, came from the back of the church is an expensive Burberry suit with gold cuff links. His wavy hair had specks of gray in it. His goatee was lined nice and neat. "Son, I understand your frustration, but you are not to beat a woman in front of everybody like that. Just take a look at the pews. Look at how your family is looking at you in total fear and trepidation," he whispered.

I glanced over his shoulder and saw how my family was purposely avoiding eye contact with me. The women had their arms wrapped safely around their children. The men looked off everywhere but in my direction. I could hear Ebony's whimpering in the distance. "Yo, I don't give a fuck. That bitch brought her punk ass in here and disrespected me in front of my people. She lucky I ain't kill her ass on everything. So I don't want to hear that shit, Pop. Word up."

My old man frowned his face and ran his fingers through his hair. "I want to have a sit down with you and your brothers tomorrow at my mansion in Bayside. We have some very important things to go over. I'll expect you to be there, Mijo."

Mijo meant my son in Spanish. My father had a habit of calling me and my brothers this. He also never spoke English unless he had to which was rare. "I think I might need more than a day to get my head right. Today is Wednesday. Why don't you give me until Friday and I should be good to go?"

I looked over my baby lying in his coffin and felt like throwing up. I needed a fix. That heroin was calling me like never before. I could feel my veins throbbing in my arms. My father nodded. "Okay, Mijo. That's understandable, but you make sure that you're there Friday. Get your head together. I have some heavy news that I'll be dropping on you kids. You'll need your strength." He kissed me on both cheeks and walked away. I placed my hand onto my son's chest and shook my head. I was missing him like crazy.

* * *

I didn't make it home until eleven o'clock that night. As soon as I stepped foot in the door, I started to take off of my clothes and headed toward my master bedroom so I could grab my dope out of the bottom drawer dresser. I loosened my tie and dropped it on the carpet. Tori carne out of the kitchen with an apron around her waist. She wiped her hands on it.

"Baby, I'm so glad that you're home. I was worried sick about you." She ran up to me and wrapped her arms around my neck. After I slapped Ebony's ass around a little bit, Tori had driven her home. By the time she got back to the church, we'd gon' to the cemetery to put Maine into the ground. Nobody was allowed to witness the burial of him other than the men of our family. It was a Vega's custom.

"Yo, I'm good, but I need my shit. I'm feening. My stomach feel like it's being ripped out of me."

I moved her out of my way and rushed into the bedroom. Dropping to my knees and pulling out the lower drawer, I took a half kilo of heroin out of it and sat it on top of my dresser. I opened it and took some of the powder, placing it in the palm of my hand, snorting it hard. On contact, the drug rushed to my brain, sending bells that rang inside of my ears. My entire head became numb, then the feeling coursed its way throughout my entire body until I got that euphoric feeling of happiness. I held my nose and closed my eyes.

It felt like I was being pulled backward. There was a constant drip in the back of my throat and every it time it happened, I felt higher and higher. My penis got hard. I grabbed it and squeezed it. Tori came into the room and looked up to me.

"Do you feel better now, daddy?" she asked, placing her hand on my chest. I nodded.

"A little, but you know what you can do to help daddy take his mind off of this evening?" I asked, looking down on her and setting the dope back on my dresser as I closed the package. She dropped to her knees and rubbed up and down my pants front.

"I already know, daddy, and I got you." She unzipped my pants and pulled my dick out, stroking it up and down in her small hand. She kissed the head and trailed her tongue all around it, before sucking it into her mouth.

The insides of her mouth felt hot and wet. Her suction was amazing. I could feel her tongue licking all around my helmet. Tori was my baby mother's youngest sister, and in my opinion, the coldest out of all of them. She was five feet six inches tall, caramel-skinned with light freckles all over her pretty face. She had pure brown eyes and a body of a goddess. She was my in-house pussy.

I had a some feelings for her, but no love just yet. I wouldn't let nobody hurt her and as long as she was under my wing, I felt it was my job to spoil her, but that was as far as it went. I didn't think there was a woman on earth that could lock me down. I loved pussy way too much.

I grabbed a handful of her hair and humped into her mouth as she squeezed her lips together and pumped my dick up and down with blazing speed. Her jaws hollowed in and out. She slurped at my pole loudly with her eyes closed. She looked like a fine ass porn star. "Yo, stop playin' wit' me and take them hands away. You know I don't play that shit. You suck daddy with mouth and tongue only."

I gasped, losing my breath. Her head was bomb when she didn't use her fists. I needed that straight ho' to come out of her. She popped me out with a loud thawk! "I'm sorry, daddy, but I got you. Let's get it."

She sucked me back into her mouth and put her hands behind her back, spearing her head into my lap like a savage. Her spit dripped off of my balls and landed on the carpet in my master bedroom. I humped into her mouth, tightening my grip in her hair. "Uh. Uh. Uh. Uh. Yeah, boo. That's daddy's baby right there. Suck me, ma. Let me cum all in it. Shit, this mouth."

I closed my eyes tighter and sped up my pace. My dick traveled all the way down her throat before I pulled it back only to invade her esophagus again. Her mouth traveled up and down my penis. She nipped at the head with her teeth and sent shivers throughout my body. I had to hold on to the dresser to maintain my balance.

I tried to lose myself within the bliss of her head game, but my son's face continued to pop into my head, preventing me from doing so. I could feel the dope heightening the senses of my pipe. I pulled it out of her mouth and noted she kept on sucking at the air for a split second until she carne to her senses.

"Baby, I gotta hit that pussy. I need to fuck something hard. You hear me?" I asked, picking her up and tossing her onto the bed before yanking her black Prada skirt up her thick thighs.

She opened them wide and ran her fingers up and down her slit. She wore pink panties that were silk and nearly see through. I could make out the wet spot on the center of them. "Okay, daddy. We can do whatever you want. Just tell me how you need me. I'll do whatever you want. I belong to you."

She pulled her panties to the side of her pussy, exposing the meaty brown lips. A clear gel seeped out of them. I stuck my face between her legs and sucked both lips into my mouth like a vacuum cleaner. Her pussy tasted sweet with a hint of salt. I ran my tongue up and down her crease, then slid it into her hole, flicking it like crazy. She bucked her hips and sat all the way up on the bed before falling backwards.

"Daddy! Oh my, daddy," she moaned and opened her thighs wider. She lowered the straps on her dress and her breasts came bouncing out with erect dark brown nipples that looked like bigger versions of Hershey Kisses. I watched her pull on them and push her mounds together. I opened her pussy lips wider with my thumbs, then licked all around her clit before trapping it with my teeth.

I flicked it with my tongue. Her juices rushed out of her and dripped down my neck. Her scent was strong. It drove me crazy. "Aww, daddy! Daddy! Get up here and fuck yo' baby! Please! I need that dick! Please, daddy!" she begged.

I licked up and down her thick thighs and bit into them, sucking them with my lips. I could taste her perfume that she may have sprayed on them before she left the house that day. I ran my tongue all the way back up to her clit and nipped at it. I slid two fingers into her pussy, running them in and out at full speed. I needed to taste her cum. I needed to swallow her juices. It riled me up every single time. Pussy juice was like my spinach. I used it for fuel to go ape shit crazy.

"Suck my clit, daddy! Suck my clit like that! Aww, fuck! Aww fuck, daddy! I'm cumming. Yo' baby cumming!" she screamed, before shaking like crazy. I continued to suck and finger her. I swallowed as much of her juices as I could, while I trapped her vagina's nipple and sucked on it for all it was worth. She wrapped her thighs around my head and came and came, smearing my face with her creams.

I hopped between her legs and ran my big dick head up and down her dripping slit. The head slipped into her pink hole. I slammed forward and buried my dick as deep into her as it could go. I was trying to bump one of her ovaries.

"Aww, shit! Daddy, it's deep. Holy fuck! Hit this cat, daddy! Hit it right." She tossed the back of her thighs on my shoulders. I got to banging that pussy like it was my last piece on earth. My hips popped forward and back with blazing speed. Her walls sucked at me and tried to keep me in every time I pulled back. She was scorching on the inside and tight. Her scent wafted up my nose, fueling the best within.

"Uh. Uh. Uh. Yeah, ma. This daddy's. This daddy's. I'm fucking my lil' one," I growled, hitting that ass off right. The headboard slammed into the wall repeatedly. We bounced up and down in the bed. The springs were squeaking like we were jumping all around on top of it. I could feel the fan from the nightstand blowing on my chest and the sweat sliding down the side of my face.

"Uh. Uh. daddy. Ooh shit, daddy! My stomach, my stomach. You're in my stomach! Aww, shit!" she screamed and ran her tongue all over her lips.

I tossed her legs down and leaned forward, sucking all over her big titties. I sucked on the nipples while my hips continued to pound into her. It felt like I was fucking a velvet drain that felt soft and oozed out thick bubbles of her juices.

I sucked on her neck and fucked her as hard as I could. "I'm about to cum, ma. Daddy's 'bout to cum. Aww fuck, babe."

I felt my entire body tingling. My head got sensitive before it expanded and my nut shot out of me. My balls rose into my lower abs as I released squirt after squirt into her hot pussy. All the while I bit into her neck like a vampire. She bucked under me and ran her hands all over my back. She sucked my ear lobe into her ear and moaned. "I love you, daddy. I love you so much."

I flipped her to her stomach and kissed all over that fat ass booty. I opened the cheeks and licked up and down her crease, taking my time as I sucked on her crinkle back there. I looked at how thick my baby was. I couldn't get enough of her body.

T.J. Edwards

# Chapter 3

I waited until nine o'clock at night the following Friday before I showed up at my old man's mansion out in Bayside. I really didn't feel like fucking with him or my brothers. I was missing my son and my right hand woman, Eve. She had committed suicide only a month prior to my son's murder. My head was fucked up, and I didn't feel like being passive nor subordinate to my father. I was ready to kill up some shit.

My uncle Javier answered the door to my father's mansion with two old school, Cuban bodyguards standing behind him. Both were armed and I knew that on my father's command, that they'd murder something quickly. "Juanito, my nephew. It's about time you showed up. It's good to see you." He pulled me in for an embrace. I wrapped my arms around him briefly. I wasn't into that affectionate shit with other men. I didn't give a fuck if they were my blood relatives or not. It just wasn't in me. But with bitches, it was a different story.

"Yo, I'm here, Unc. Let's get this shit over and done with. I got other places to be." I walked past him and into the mansion.

Everywhere I looked inside of the palace, I spotted an armed guard pacing the expanse of the mansion. They had scowls on their faces on high alert. I was guessing that since my father had fully taken a hold of the Vega fields that my family back home in Havana must of felt he needed twenty-four hour protection. It made sense to me.

I walked past the grand living room with the crystal chandeliers and the Maplewood fully glossed tables. Marble floors and counter tops too, nodding my head. My pops definitely had major swag in my opinion. All around the mansion were pictures of famous Cuban leaders throughout history.

Javier led me downstairs and into the den where I saw my little brothers, Miguel and Tristian, sitting at the long table that my father had inside of his den. Along with them were bodyguards and my father's personal attorney and right hand man, Shapiro. Miguel and I shared the same parents. He was four years younger than me. Out of all of my father's children, he was the one that looked most like him.

He had wavy hair, light brown eyes, and fair skin. He and I had a decent relationship. I loved him because he was my brother. I would never allow anything to happen to him while I was present. But then again, we didn't have that type of relationship where I would go above and beyond for him under any circumstances. We were siblings and that was that.

I found an empty chair and pulled it out, taking my place. I could still feel the effects of the drug running rampant in my system. My eyes were low and my nose felt like it wanted to drool. I dabbed at it with a Kleenex and sat my right hand on the table looking at the front of the room where my father sat with a look of frustration.

"How nice of you to join us, Juanito. Now that you're here, we can begin." He stood up and nodded at Shapiro. Shapiro was a sharp, well-dressed Italian with wavy black hair and green eyes. He was about five feet six inches tall with a sharp nose. He and my father had been rocking for more than twenty years. I'd forgotten how they'd linked up to begin with, but ever since they had, they'd been as thick as thieves.

When it came to the affairs of the Vegas, Shapiro was the man that took care of everything from the inside out. "As you all should know, it has taken quite a lump sum to make this ordeal that took place with Maine Vega go away. There is a little girl that is still in the hospital fighting for her life. In addition to that, we had to answer for Tristian's wounds and the other person that was killed at the same time all of this took place.

Now it wasn't easy, but thankfully, we were able to buy a Senator before all of this took place. And the Vegas have promised to see to it that he becomes Mayor of New York. I am confident with the right strings being pulled, we can make this happen." Shapiro stepped to his left and placed his hand on my father's shoulder. "Sir?"

My father looked down the table at me and then to my brothers. "Sons, that is not the only reason that you've been called here tonight. There are actually two very important reasons. For the first one, I'll show you a video."

The lights were dimmed before he stood up and rolled down his projector. Seconds later, the film was rolling. I saw my Porsche pulling into the parking lot across from Flex and his crew. As soon as I saw where this video was going, I lowered my head. It was just like my old man to obtain footage for shit that others never had access to.

Just hearing the "oohs" and "ahhs" in the room made me sick to my stomach. I raised my head just in time for me to see Flex roll up on Maine and gun him down with a big smile on his face. His Escalade then stormed out of the parking lot. I could see myself running toward Maine, but it was too late. He was already gone by the time I made it back to him. I felt like shit. I jumped up and made my way out of the door.

"Man, fuck this shit. I'm out of here." Two of my father's armed guards blocked my path, breathing down on me as if they were ready to send me to the reaper. I was seconds away from losing my cool.

"Sit your ass down, Juanito! Now! You are apart of this family whether you like it or not. Sit down!" he hollered from across the room, flicking the lights on.

I stood there for a minute, the whole image of seeing my son's murder in front of me fresh in my mind. I felt like snapping. I knew that I had to kill Flex fast or I was going to lose my mind. I made my way back to my seat and reluctantly sat down.

"Now, what that video shows is that you were negligent. You kicked off a bunch of bullshit with my grandson in the car. It shouldn't have happened. It was less than smart. You are the oldest son that I have. I expect more from you. Do you understand that?" he hollered.

I ain't feel like giving him a response, so I didn't. I didn't like no muthafucka hollering at me. I didn't care who they were. Even though he was my father, I didn't feel like he had the right to raise his voice at me. It was taking all of the will power deep within my soul for me not to go ballistic and suffer the consequences later.

"Yo, Pop, I feel you. But can you stop coming at me like I'm some fucking kid? No matter what that video showed, I lost my son that day. That shit is eating at me. So there is nothing that you're going to say or do that will discipline me worse than life already has. Nah' mean?" I pulled my nose and sniffed loudly.

Instead of giving me a response, he exhaled loudly and shook his head. "That brings me to the second part of our meeting today. I am saddened to inform you kids that I have pancreatic cancer. The doctors have given me a few more months to live. I may be able to get six at the most. Due to this unfortunate circumstance, I will be naming one of you as my successor."

He sat in his chair and looked all of us over. The news was devastating enough. I mean I knew that my mother had confessed to me that she'd been poisoning his food for some time now, but to see that it actually worked was mind boggling.

She'd always said that whenever my father stepped down from our family's business, I was supposed to step up on his throne. That it was my birthright, and as much as I felt I didn't need him to become great, I agreed with what she'd spoken. I jumped up and shook my head.

"What do you mean one of us will be named your successor? I'm the oldest. It's my birthright and you can't take that away from me. No one can!" I snapped.

"Sit down, Juanito. Your actions with this past event have made me doubtful in your ability to rule this family once I am gone. I have very little faith in

33

you. You're much too impulsive. You could cause this family to crash fast and hard. So, I will not just hand you anything. I have a contest for the three of you."

"Yo, nah. We ain't doing no contest. It's my birthright, Pops. You can't do this shit." I was getting more and more heated to the point I wanted to start shooting up in that piece. I saw myself knocking my pop's head off, then murking his right hand man before having a major shoot out with his guards. I was feeling kamikaze as fuck.

"Sit down, Juanito! I will not tell you again!" my father snapped. He stood up and slammed his big hand down on the table. His face was beet red. I took my seat and looked across the table at my brother, Tristian. He had tears in his eyes. He wiped them away and frowned his face.

"Pop, when did you find this out? And why did you wait so long to tell us that you were dying?" he asked, getting up and giving our father a hug.

He was so soft to me. I wasn't feeling any of those emotions he had. I don't think that Miguel was either, but I wasn't sure. I sat back in my seat and lowered my head. Now I'd have to compete with my brothers for my own birthright. It was insulting. I had visions of killing the both of them. *Boom. Boom.* Competition over with.

They hugged for what seemed like an eternity. "I told you kids once I was able to live with the results. I have been working over time to get this family into a stable position. Senator Jefferey Grant will take our family to the next level. With him in power as mayor, we will have a direct line to distribute our heroin and cocaine all throughout the United States from right here in New York City.

We'll be able to move freely, sons. That means millions and millions of dollars for all of you.

The person that takes my throne must always make sure that our homeland is the first place that is always taken care of. Without Havana and our fields, there is no Vegas. Understand that."

I lowered my head and curled my lip. I needed to get the fuck out of there. I was getting more and more angry.

"So, what is the competition?" I asked, trying to sound as calm as possible. The lights flipped back off and he flipped on the projector. This time there was an aerial view of the Red Hook Housing Projects out in South Brooklyn. It was a view of them from the past winter I surmised because there was snow everywhere.

"This is the destination for us Vegas to conquer. If we can fully take over these houses, even before Senator Grant comes into office as mayor of the city, we can look to make five million dollars a day from both our coke and heroin through these housing projects.

Right now as it stands, this area is the cocaine capitol of America. We want to make them also the heroin capitol, as well. The first one of you that can conquer this area and bring me fifteen million dollars to go towards Senator Grant's campaign will step upon my throne to rule as king of the Vegas. You have three months to make this happen."

I jumped up. "Is that all'?" I asked, looking down on him.

"Oh, so you think you can conquer so easily, Juanito? I'll have you to know that currently they are ran by the enemies of the Vegas. Mr. Bruno Gomez himself and the Gomez family have stated their claim to these houses. Not only that, but these houses are flooded with the cocaine that comes directly from the Gomez's cocaine fields in Havana. Bruno has had a lock on them for nearly five years now. The residents pledge their loyalties to him and his sons, Wisin and Chulo. I'd like for you to tell me how you'll be able to take them over so easily?" he challenged me.

"The price is fifteen million and the Red Hook Houses. It's all I need to know. My birthright is on the line right now. That's what matters to me and nothing more at this juncture."

"Alright then, Mijo. You're dismissed. So are the rest of you. I am here for anyone of you that needs me to mentor him in this endeavor. I love all three of you and be safe out there."

I made my way out of his house with my brothers calling my name. I ignored the both of them. That night, I grabbed me a bottle of Hornitos and found myself sitting with my back against Evelina's grave.

Evelina had been my best friend, right hand woman, and the heart and soul of me for as long as I could remember. That was until she'd taken her life about a half of year ago right in front of me. I was missing her like crazy and needed her more than I could ever remember. I took the bottle of Hornitos and turned it all the way up, swallowing the liquor in big gulps, before holding it at my side with my eyes closed.

"I miss you, Eve. I wish I could hold yo' lil' fine ass right now. I hope you looking over Maine up there. Tell him that I'm sorry. That I should have been a better father. I should have protected him more. But I will not rest soundly until I bring his killer to justice. Street justice, that is."

I took another swallow from the bottle, almost killing it. "Tell Punkin I said fuck her. I know she up there talking a bunch of shit about the way I cared for our son. But tell that bitch I said fuck her. I don't feel like she could have done a better job. In fact, I'm sure of it."

I opened my eyes as the wind began to blow in the night. The sounds of crickets were loud in my ears. The graveyard looked dreary and even a bit scary like something straight out of a horror movie. Eve's grave was located directly in the middle of it, as well. I didn't have any problem making it to her grave, but now that I was so drunk, I didn't know how the fuck I was going to get up out of there. I turned the Hornitos up and drank as much as I could.

"This punk muthafucka got the nerve to put my birth right up for grabs like I'm some bitch or something. I'm the first born. That seat is supposed to be mine and not nobody else's. I'd murder Tristian and Miguel's bitch ass before I let them take my throne. Word is bond. They don't wanna fuck wit' the Showbiz kid. That's on my mother!" I hollered, feeling myself get vexed.

I turned my head around and kissed her tombstone. "You were my only love, Eve. I ain't never care about nobody outside of my mother like I did you. I wish you would have come to me before you made up your mind. You'd still be in this fight wit' me right now. We'd have no problem taking over them Projects. I'm confident in that. You're still my every thing, Boo. Word up."

I kissed the tombstone again and laid my head up against it. I could see her beautiful face in my mind. I wished that I could kiss her perfect lips again. Eve was my world. I saw that now. She was my better half and I felt like I needed her more than I'd ever have before. I don't know how it happened, but I wound up passing out with my face against her tombstone, missing her like crazy. I didn't awake until the next afternoon, and when I did, I had a thousand Army ants crawling all over me.

# Chapter 4

It was a week after my father's meeting. I sat across the table from Veeto, Eve's uncle. I would hit licks for him. He would pay me twenty five thousand dollars apiece for each person that I slumped. He slammed a map down in front of me and said, "Son, I hate them punk ass Gomezes, kid. Word is bond. Here go all of the information you'll need on Chulo and Wisin's bitch ass. Yo, if you wind up whacking them fuck boys, I'll throw you thirty gees just on the strength.

Oh, and here go that info you needed on Flex, too. I got the low down on where his sister stays. They supposed to be throwing a party for his birthday out in Brooklyn. I guess them Harlem niggas finally ran him out of their borough. Anyway, it's already a fifty thousand dollar bounty on his head from the gods out in Harlem. I know it ain't about the money for you, but once you whack his punk ass, I'ma collect the money and make sure you get it anyway." He leaned across the table and we hugged.

"I'm sorry to hear about your kid too, boss. If there is anything the god can do, just let me know."

I nodded my head and left from his crib, feeling like I'd made some progress. It took me a minute to drive away from in front of his spot because my head was spinning like crazy. Anytime I dealt with anybody that me and Eve were accustomed to dealing with, it made me miss her like crazy.

I got to hearing her voice and laughter in my head. It was getting to the point that it was driving me crazy. I pulled the aluminum-foiled package of heroin out of my pocket and opened it. I lowered my head and tooted about a gram up each nostril. I waited for the effects of the drug to take over me, but it was to the point where it wasn't hitting me like it once had.

The tooting thing was getting old. I needed to ingest the drug through my veins. I knew it would be the only way it would do anything for me. I was just kind of scared of what that meant for the future. I couldn't see myself sticking a syringe in my veins. It just wasn't me.

So I tooted another gram before I pulled from in front of Veeto's crib, feeling the slight effects of the Vega's heroin that was more than ninety five percent pure.

\* \* \*

Ten minutes later, I was beating on Tristian's door to his crib out in Brooklyn. I just needed to pick his brain to see how much he really wanted our father's throne. He'd always been one of those niggas that couldn't see himself staying in the hood. He wanted to venture out to do bigger and better things. He was a college boy.

I didn't think that our father's drug empire lined up with what he saw for his future. If that was the case, then I was cool with that. But if he was thinking of actually going for the throne, then I had thoughts of putting two in his melon and tossing him over the Brooklyn bridge with no mercy or remorse.

This shit was real to me. I didn't give a fuck if he was my paternal brother or not. I was born to be king.

So I beat on his door harder and waited for him to answer it. About thirty seconds later, he did and with a crazy look on his face.

"Damn nigga, why the fuck you beating on my door like you Twelve or something?" he asked, stepping to the side.

I walked past him and into the house. The heat hit me at once and boosted the high the heroin had given me. "Yo, I come to fuck wit' you for a minute. I want you to rollout wit' me so we can handle some bitness together, too."

I looked around his pad and saw Kalani looking at us from the kitchen. She smiled at me and waved. Tristian closed the door and scratched his head. "Yo, what you talking about, kid? About a week ago after Pops ended the meeting, you acted like you ain't wanna fuck with the god. Now you're back up and talking and shit." He shook his head. "Yo, you gotta get on some kind of Lithium or something. Word up."

He sat on the love seat and pointed to the couch across from him. "Have a seat, son."

I sat down and pulled my nose. I needed another fix already. I felt my high going down for some reason. My head began to hurt. I think it was the heat. First, it had boosted my high and then it felt like it was taking it away. Maybe I did need Lithium.

"Nah son, peep. I got the four one one on where that fuck nigga Flex gon' be tonight. I wanna roll over there and knock his brains out of his head, then kill whoever in the house along with him in honor of my son. I aint been able to sleep every since he killed Maine. It's fucking me up, Dunn." I ran my hand I over my face in mounting frustration. "So you gon' fuck wit me or not?" I asked ready to get up and walk out of his crib.

Had he said n'all, I was gon' come back and murder him in cold blood. I was already irritated that he and my father acted like I didn't have a reason to be heated over what had taken place with my son and my birthright. He nodded his head.

"Let me grab a shower real fast and I'll be right out to fuck wit' you. Just chill here. You want something to eat or snack on?" he asked, stopping in the doorway.

"Yeah, let me get one of them Tahitian Treats you keep in your fridge and some cookies or something. I got a sweet tooth."

"I got you. I'ma have Kalani get you right while I jump in the shower." He left from the doorway and I pulled out my phone to look over my messages. I had three from Wetto with dollar signs attached to them. I was guessing the homey was in need of more product.

I had intentions on getting up with him as soon as I finished handling Flex's bitch ass. There was also another message from Veeto telling me to call him urgently. This one I responded to right away. He picked up on the first ring.

"Kid, I got you all set up. The lil' bitch Mandy gon' meet you at the front door. Y'all went to school together. She familiar with you and she know what's good. However, she can't leave away from that situation, so make sure you handle that. Nah' mean?"

"Got you, Blood. I'll catch you later. Love you, kid." I ended the call and put my phone back up. My brother's bitch, Kalani, stepped into the room with a plate full of chocolate chip cookies and a bottle of Fruit Punch Tahitian Treat. She sat them on the table.

"Tristian told me to bring you these. How are you holding up?" She was dressed in a short pink Fendi skirt and belly shirt that showcased her belly button ring.

"Where my brother at?" I asked, ignoring her question.

"He just got into the shower. He said he'll be out in ten minutes. Now, how are you doing?" She looked down at me with her big brown eyes, concerned.

I grabbed her by the wrist and slid my hand between her thick thighs. I ran it all the way up until my fingers brushed her panty front. "Damn, that go there that fat thang right there." I squeezed the lips together through the panties and bit into my bottom lip. This woman was so fucking bad. She moaned and tried to yank her wrist away from me.

"Stop, Showbiz. You said we wasn't gon' do nothing like this no more. I believed you. You know I love your brother."

I reached both of my hands under her skirt and pulled her to me, using of her ass cheeks. Once in front of my face, I slipped my head under her skirt and licked the crotch of her panties, searching for her taste. I licked up and down her material, before kissing all over her thick thighs.

"Stop, Showbiz. You gon' get us in trouble. Damn," she whimpered, looking over my shoulder in the direction of the back of the house where Tristian was showering. I pulled her crotch band all the way to the side and exposed her pussy lips, before sucking them into my mouth. I slobbered all over them in a hunger-like way.

She humped into my face. Threw her head back. "Aww, fuck. You ain't right. I swear you ain't right."

I had her lips wide open, sliding my tongue in and out of her at full speed. I loved making a bitch do what she knew she shouldn't be doing. I knew she loved my brother with all of her heart, but I didn't give a fuck. She was too bad. I wanted to fuck and touch all over her whenever I wanted to. I didn't give a fuck how Tristian or nobody else felt about it either. I thought as her juices spilled onto my tongue. I slipped a finger inside of her and gripped her ass. The bathroom door opened. She pushed me away and pulled her skirt down, rushing out of the room on weak legs.

"Damn, Showbiz. You gotta stay away from me." She disappeared to the back of the house. I sucked my fingers and laughed to myself. I picked up one of the cookies and ate it.

* * *

I handed Tristian a pistol and watched him tuck it under his shirt in the small of his back. He had his ski mask on top of his head ready to be pulled down.

"Let's handle this bitness, nigga. Fuck is you waiting on?" he asked, looking me over closely. I'd paused for a minute because my heart was beating super fast. I was having a hard time breathing and I almost panicked. I wasn't trying to go back to the hospital from another overdose.

The last one had taken so much out of me that I thought I was going to die. Just imagining me going through that shit again was enough to freak me out. I couldn't let my brother see no weakness in me, so I played it off. I screwed the silencer into my .40 Glock and slid it into my pants. I pulled my mask down over my face and stepped into the cool night air. The entire block was completely darkened as if somebody had shot out the street lights.

"Come on, lets go." We ran down the alley and through the back yard of the brownstone. Once there, I found the number for Mandy that Veeto had texted to me. I texted her and told her to bring her ass down stairs before I deleted her number from my phone.

I could hear the music coming from upstairs. They were banging Pusha T's album. I heard lots of I laughter. I could tell that they were enjoying themselves. For some reason, I took offense to that.

Mandy came down the stairs and answered the door about a minute later. When she opened the door, I could hear the music as clear as day coming from the inside. She stepped outside with us and closed the door. She held out her arms for me to step into them.

"What's good, Showbiz? Veeto already told me what was good. I'm sorry to hear about your son, boss." She hugged me tightly, before taking a step back.

"I appreciate that. So where is this nigga at?" I asked, growing impatient. I was ready to kill his bitch ass so I could get some sleep. Then I could focus on everything surrounding the Gomez's and my father's throne.

I couldn't for the life of me come up with a strategy. I hadn't slept for more than few hours at a time with the exception of when I passed out on Eve's grave. But even then, it was one of those uncomfortable sleeps.

"Yo, so you go straight up the stairs and then to your right. That nigga Flex and two of his homies, along with three of my stripper friends gon' be right there. When I stepped out, he was getting a lap dance by the living room with my friend, Trinity. We worked at the same club together. Girl got some skills."

"Bitch, I don't wanna hear all that. Finish with what you was saying!" I snapped ready to choke her ass out. She rolled her eyes.

"Anyway, that's where he is. You gotta get up there so y'all can do your thing. Come on, I'll show you the way. I don't like this pancake ass nigga. First, he was repping Harlem. Now all a sudden, he's one of Brooklyn's finest."

She opened the door and waved at us to follow her. I looked down and saw that this Puerto Rican bitch had a fat ass booty like she was straight from the Projects. That muhfucka was jiggling and everything. I felt crazy ass hell having a hard on on my way to kill up some shit, but I did.

She took one step after the next. When we made it to the top, I saw where the door was. She put her finger to her lips. "A'ight, let me stick my head in there to make sure that everything is as it was before I left." She held up one finger. I looked back at Tristian. His light brown eyes were bucked in the mask. I wondered if he was scared for his life.

I'd always took him to be one of them soft ass niggas anyway. He definitely wasn't about that life like I was. I didn't know how my father could even put his throne up for grabs. It was clear that I was the only one fit to have it. Mandy pulled her head back out of the door and smiled.

"Yep, they still over there doing exactly what they before I left. You good. Just make sure y'all don't hit of my girls."

I nodded and stepped up to her. I grabbed her by the throat, pulled out my Glock and slammed the barrel into her eye, then carried her part way down the stairs before pulling the trigger. Her head jerked violently. She fell to the ground with blood rushing out of her like a spilled can of paint. Tristian jumped back. I moved him out of the way as I took the stairs two at a time.

"Let's go, nigga."

I pulled the mask up and saw a bunch of purses piled in one chair of the dining room. On the table was a bunch of food and drinks. There was a big birthday cake in the middle of it, as well. I rushed inside and to my right. There were two strippers with their hands on the carpet making their asses pop up and down.

Two of Flex's men threw one dollar bills on top of them. Flex and another man sat on the couch with women on top of their laps, grinding for the fist full of hundred dollar bills that he had in his right hand. As soon as I saw him, I pulled my mask off.

Something must have told him to look up, because as soon as my mask was off, he looked toward me. His eyes bucked. He tried to throw the stripper that was on his lap off of him, taking the .9 millimeter Beretta out of his waistband. But it was too late.

I rushed him with my Glock out, stepping on one of the strippers hands as I made my way to him. I leveled my gun as the image of Maine's head being blown off by him came into my mind. I scrunched my face and pulled the trigger repeatedly.

The silencer made a soft, *whomp, whomp, whomp, whomp* sound as my bullets entered into his face, punching massive hole into it, knocking away large chunks of his muscles and tissues. He fell forward on the couch with his Ramen Noodles leaking out of his skull. It smelled like spoiled milk mixed with hot copper.

The stripper that had been on his lap screamed and put up her hands to block her face. More visions of Maine's murder entered into my head. How dare she celebrate the nigga that had killed my son? I hated her and all of them just like I did Flex in that moment. I placed my barrel to the back of her head and pulled the trigger, killing her.

I turned my gun on Flex's two homies who'd tried to flee from the living room. My bullets wet their backs up, dropping them to the floor.

I made it back to the living room to see two of the strippers hiding behind the couch, shaking uncontrollably. Scared of the unknown. Knowing their fate lied in the hands of a stranger.

"Ahhhh!" The screamed out in unison.

There was no way I could leave them alive.

I imagined Maine taking the bullets from Flex's gun again. I bit into my bottom lip and bucked them both two times a piece, blowing their heads back off the couch and all against the wall. I took a step back with my smoking gun and looked around. Tristian was in the middle of the floor with a dazed expression. "Nigga, tear this muhfucka up and make sure ain't nobody else here. Come on. We been in here long enough!" I ordered.

I ran from the dining room into the back of the house, flipping over beds and knocking over the dressers. I searched in closets and the bathroom. Luckily, I wasn't able to find anybody else. I ran from the bathroom back into the kitchen just as Tristian was closing the door to the pantry. That made me suspicious.

"Yo, what the fuck is in there, Dunn?" I asked, walking toward it. He shook his head.

"Ah, nothing. Come on, we're good. Let's get the fuck out of here." He waved me off and made it seem like he was about to run. I waited right until he moved just enough for me to slip past him. As soon as he did, I ran to the pantry and threw open the door.

Inside of it were two females hugged up, sitting on the floor with tears running down their cheeks. One looked to be on her upper twenties, the other in her teens. I didn't give a fuck. I aimed my pistol and got ready to pull the trigger when Tristian pushed my arm out of the way.

My gun went off. The bullet crashed into a bag of flour, causing it to explode. It rained down on the ladies, turning them white.

"Nigga, what the fuck is wrong with you?" I hollered, before aiming again and pulling the trigger. It clicked repeatedly.

"Bruh, we ain't gotta kill them. It's good. We got dude's bitch ass. We can get up out of here. Come on." He tired to pull me by the sleeve of my hoodie. I yanked away from him.

"Get the fuck off of me and give me your gun. These bitches gotta die!" I reached for his pistol. He jumped back and shook his head.

"N'all, nigga. Let's go. Fuck them!" He jogged toward the doorway of the kitchen. "You coming?"

I was ready to blow my lid. The females whimpered with tears running down their cheeks. They looked helpless and weak. I wanted to slump them on the strength of them looking so fucking vulnerable. I knew that Eve would have never went out crying or begging for her life. They were disgrace to me.

On top of that, they represented a part of the mission that was incomplete. I was glad that after I'd smoked the people in the living room, that I'd pulled my mask back down because it was looked like Tristian wasn't about to give me his pistol. That made me want to go on a rampage.

I thought about grabbing a knife and stabbing them to death, but then I heard the sirens. That caused me to panic again. "Fuck! Yo, you's a bitch ass nigga for this, bruh."

I rushed out of the kitchen and to the front door, pulled it open and ran down the stairs at full speed, only stopping once to jump over Mandy's dead body before I was out into the night with Tristian on my heels. A few minutes later, we made it to the whip I'd copped to handle this business. Once we were both in, I peeled out and away from the scene.

"Yo, that's my bad, Showbiz, but them broads ain't have to die. We'd already taken care of business. Nah' mean?"

"Yo, on my word, son, that was some bitch shit. Man, if you weren't my brother, I'd be putting a bunch in you right now. That's my word. You too fucking soft with them hoes, nigga. You act like you scared to kill a bitch or something. Not knowing them hoes will kill you quick as a muthafucka. Don't you see how that Rican bitch just set that nigga Flex up to meet his end? That's what hoes do, nigga. Get that shit through yo fucking head!"

"Nigga, calm yo' ass down. One of them broads looked familiar to me. Do you remember that lil' girl that got popped the same time Maine did?" he asked.

I made a left and stopped at a red light. "Yeah, what about her?" I asked, mugging him with anger.

"Well I'm pretty sure that was her mother back there. If so, don't you think that she's been through enough?"

"Nigga, my muthafucking son lying in the dirt after being riddled with bullets and you asking me if I feel some type of way about a bitch who still got her child?" I popped the lock on his door.

"Bruh, I ain't saying it like that. I'm saying—"

"Nigga get the fuck out my whip right now!" I snapped, reaching across his lap and throwing open the door. "Get the fuck out. I swear to God one of these days the lil' blood that we share ain't gon' mean shit to me. Step!"

"Yo, you about to put me out in the middle of Brooklyn, son?" he asked, stepping one foot out of the car.

"Get the fuck out of my whip, nigga. I ain't gone say it again." I eyed him closely, ready to turn my pistol and buss him over the head with it.

He stepped out, slamming the door. "Fuck you then, Showbiz. You dirty ass nigga."

I stormed away from his soft ass and pulled on the highway with heroin on my mind.

# Chapter 5

I walked around the pile of tin foiled packages with a hundred and fifty kilos of heroin in all. At fifty gees a piece, I was looking to make a quick ten million dollars in cash. With that ten, I was thinking of putting six of it aside to go towards the fifteen million my pops said he needed in order for me to obtain his throne.

My uncle Javier had the shipment sent to me that morning. Wetto picked up one of the kilos and set it on the table that was set up in the basement. He opened it, and placed a snidbit on his pocket knife, before tooting it up his nose. He snorted hard and swallowed, holding his nose. I stood back and watched him, waiting for his reaction.

I'd already tried a gram of it before I'd called him over. I knew it was fire. I was high as a kite. My nose kept on running, so I was dabbing at it with a handkerchief. He nodded his head.

"Yeah, son, this that deal right here. I can see my cousin 'nem out in Harlem fucking wit' this product real tough. I already know the hypes out in Harlem gone go crazy over it. We doing the same thing right. Fifty a piece?"

Wetto was a heavy set Cuban nigga with tats. He was well respected in Harlem, both on his Spanish side and the Black side. Through him, I was able to funnel my dope into Harlem without really getting my hands dirty. He was a Blood nigga just like me. Back in the day, his brother and I used to hit major licks together until I had to smoke him for leaving a nigga alive who would've later came back to shoot me up.

"Yeah, son. Fifty a piece. You already know what it is," I said, walking over to him with my hand extended. He smacked it away and upped a .9 millimeter with an extended clip.

"Nah, son. I don't know what it is." He sucked his teeth and aimed his gun at my face. I jumped back and held my hands up.

"What the fuck all this about, bruh?" I was shocked and caught off guard Not only did I have my pistol upstairs, but I was high and my vision was fucking wit' me along with my heart. I'd just given Javier my last three million dollars to cop the shipment from the heroin buy to straighten that bill. He was going out on a limb fucking with me against the wishes of my father. I couldn't afford to screw him over or the deals. Wetto cocked his hammer.

"I'm tired of being your lackey, son. Word is bond, you wouldn't be able to move shit through Harlem without me. And you still got me paying fifty a piece for these birds. Nigga, fuck you. I gotta have all of this product. That's on my blood, nigga." He pulled out his phone and started dialing, he placed it to his ear. "Yeah, come on through this bitch. It's good."

I had visions of rushing him at full speed. Overpowering him and putting three in his face. I couldn't believe I had been so stupid to let this nigga in my crib. He knew where I laid my head and where my bitch stayed. I was stupid and deserved everything that was happening to me.

"Yo, if you feeling that fifty is too steep for your pockets, kid, we can talk about better prices. It ain't that serious."

I heard kicking on the back door. After a few more, it sounded like it caved in. The next thing I knew, I heard a bunch of footsteps, and then the basement was full with niggas that had red rags around their necks and machine guns in their hands.

"Yo, start taking these bricks upstairs and loading them into the van. Hurry the fuck up!" Wetto ordered. I stood there looking dumbfounded.

Two of the eight niggas that had come into the basement had their guns pinned on me. I could tell by the looks on their faces that they were waiting for the order to shoot me dead. I had to wiggle my way out of the jam I was in. As much as I wanted to tell them niggas to suck my dick, I couldn't be that stupid.

"Yo, it is what it is. But can you at least leave me two of them so I can work my way back up in the game. You know how it is out there." I tried to play as coy as I possibly could. Wetto laughed.

"Nall, son. I mean I can offer you position to work under me, probably put you in the projects or something working a Band-o, but far as you getting one of these, nall son. It ain't happening. Matter fact, lay yo' ass down. Now!" I knelt down reluctantly with my hands in the air.

"A'ight, boss. You got it." I crawled to my belly wit' my arms at my sides. Wetto put his knee in my back and duct taped my wrists behind my back.

"Yo, all four of them beauty shops that your bitch working, nigga we know about 'em. I got the info on where your mother stays out in Queens, too. If you try to come at any of the niggas you seen in here today, especially me, nigga we gone stank every last one of your people. The only son I ain't killing is you right now because you was one hunnit to my brother and ever since you and I been doing bitness, you been on the up and up with me.

And you're Blood. I can't kill one of my own even though you ain't never at none of the meetings or don't pay no kind of dues. That makes you rogue in my book. I got permission from up top to take yo' shit for the record." He finished taping my hands, then stepped back. "It ain't no I hard feelings, Showbiz. I hope you know that. It's just business."

I laid on my stomach in silence. I wanted to kill that nigga and every Blood nigga in the world. I knew I would carry a deep hatred in my heart for all of them, even though I'd been banging Blood every since I was nine years old.

"Yo, you ain't gotta worry about me coming at you, Blood. I can take this on the chin like a man."

He laughed. "Nigga you ain't got no choice." He slowly backed out of the basement.

"Remember, I know where your bitch works and where your mother lays her dome at. Play wit' me if you want to." He turned around and ran up the stairs. I turned on to my side fuming. I was sick to my stomach. It was only eleven in the morning and I knew that Tori never made it home from the shop until after five.

My sick was coming on, and I'd just lost a fortune. I squeezed my eyes together as the water got heavy behind them. I felt like a loser. Like the world was against me. I shook my head and tried my best to try to remain calm, drifting off to sleep.

\*\*\*

"Oh my God! Showbiz! What happened?" Tori asked, running to my aid and kneeling beside me. She pulled my wrists up to her mouth and bit at the tape before pulling out a Swiss army knife and cutting it from my wrists and ankles. I pulled it all off of me, and sat up.

"Fuck! Fuck! Fuck! Fuck!" I hollered before standing up. "That bitch nigga, Wetto, set me up baby. He just hit me for ten million dollars of product. I'm sick as hell." I placed my hands on my hips and paced back and forth. Tori covered her mouth.

"Ten million dollars worth? What are you going to do?" she asked with her eyes wide open. I shrugged my shoulders.

"I don't know, baby. I swear to God, I don't know." I fell to my knees and lowered my head. That's when the tears fell uncontrollably.

Tori knelt beside me, placing her arm around my shoulder. "I know you're going through something right now, but I just want you to know that I love you and I got ya back, baby. I'll do whatever you need me to do. I believe in you. We'll recover from this lost. All I ask is that you don't do anything stupid. Please." She rested her head onto my shoulder.

Even though those words were comforting, and I knew that they were what she was supposed to say to me at a time like this, they failed to make me feel any better. I had nothing but murder on my mind. There was no way that I was going to allow for some nigga to come into my crib and take ten million dollars of my dope. Then lay me down and bind me, so my woman could come home to release me, then laugh in my face, without me murdering every muthafucking body in his family and his blood line. What Wetto failed to realize is that I knew where his baby mother and kid stayed. I knew where his grandparents also resided.

I had visions of slicing all of them up I into itty bitty pieces and eating them as if I was a cannibal or something. I gotta get them.

"Yo, I appreciate you, ma, but right now, let me get a hold of myself." I stood up and pulled her into my arms, kissing her forehead.

* * *

Later that night, after Tori was asleep, I wound up doing something that I thought I would never do. I stepped into the bathroom and closed the door. I took off all of my clothes before sitting in a tub of hot bathwater. I exhaled loudly and laid my head back against the tiles of the wall. I stayed that way for ten minutes before getting out and drying myself off. Then I sat on the closed lid of the toilet.

I grabbed the tray of heroin and works from the sink, sitting it on my lap. I picked up the syringe that was already filled with the Vega's heroin inside of it. Wrapped the rope around my left arm, and clenched my fist over and over again until my veins popped out of my skin.

Once they were good and ready, I targeted the thick one right inside of my inner forearm, sliding the needle into it. I closed my eyes and took a deep breath. "Yo, I'm sorry, Eve."

I pushed down on the feeder, feeling the poison shoot into me. As soon as it entered my bloodstream, I felt like I was having a thousand orgasms at one time. Instead of the sound of bells that I usually got from tooting, now I heard a nice, soft, and soothing Jazz music. I was unable to feel sadness or anger. The serotonin in my brain was intensified.

I felt good, but laid back like I didn't have a care in the world. I closed my eyes, but at the same time, I was fully alert. All of my senses were heightened. I didn't need for my eyes to be open to see how I felt. The music made me feel good. I could hear each chord like never before. I felt I like a snake being charmed out on a basket.

The music called to me and made me happier than I had ever been. My dick stuck straight up into the air. It throbbed and pulsated against my stomach. It appeared to be a full eleven inches now when I was used to it being just a little under ten.

I ran my hand over my face and licked my lips. It gave me tingles. I needed to fuck something and fast. I looked over and picked up the syringe, kissing it. "Damn, Eve. I wish I would have tried this shit with you way back then. I understand why you did it this way now. I swear I do," I said out loud.

*Bang! Bang! Bang! Bang!*

I heard knocking at the door. "Baby, are you okay in there? Who are you talking to?" Tori asked through the door. I damn near jumped off the toilet, dropping the syringe to the floor.

"Aww, shit. Uh, nobody. I was praying," I lied. "Gon' back to bed. I'll be in there in a minute." I started to clean up all of the drug utensils I had spread all over the bathroom

"Baby, can you please hurry up? I need you out here with me," she whined.

"A'ight, boo. I'll be out in a minute. You got my word on that. Meet me in the bedroom. Here I come."

"But I gotta pee."

"Then use the other bathroom! Go! I'll be out in a minute.!" I snapped, feeling my blood pressure rise. "I'm finna come wax that ass anyway, Make sure my pussy clean!"

"Okay, damn!"

I could hear her bare feet walking away from the door. I closed my eyes and nodded out for a few minutes before getting up and getting myself together. I was high as a muthafucka. I knew that this was goin' to be the beginning of a beautiful relationship between me and Mrs. Heroin.

# Chapter 6

I was broke. Down and out. Javier was hitting my phone like crazy asking me about his money. I didn't have any real response to give him, so instead of picking up, I simply ignored the texts and calls.

I took a week off from life. I stayed in the crib, in the basement the entire time while Tori went off to work and tried to put a kilo of heroin into my system little by little. I stayed so high that I didn't even recognize the days as they passed by. I didn't come to my senses until the seventh day of my hiatus.

It was a Thursday night, around seven o'clock or so. Tori came running into the crib with tears in her eyes. "Showbiz! Showbiz, where are you?" she hollered.

Even though I was in the basement, I could hear her through the floor boards. I had been nodding in and out. I jerked up when I heard my name. I got myself together, went up the stairs two at a time until I was standing in front of her in the dining room. "Baby, what's the matter?" I asked, holding her by her arms.

She was dressed in a pink and black Fendi skirt suit over black red bottoms. "That dude, Wetto, came into the shop today. Him and three of his boys. They were fucking with my workers. They went from station to station, knocking over their products and being real aggressive a handsy with them. Wetto himself pulled me into my office, picked me up and sat me on my desk, before placing his forehead against mine. He was saying that from there on out, whenever any of the Bloods' women wanted their hair done, I was supposed to have my workers do their hair for free. That as long as I played ball, my shop wouldn't have anything to worry about. Then he kissed me on my lips and gone say, "I belong to the Bloods now." She lowered her head and covered her face with her hands. "All the ladies in the shop said that Wetto is crazy. I know don't want no problems with him or the Bloods. So we're just going to do their women's hair whenever they show up so he won't hurt anybody. I was terrified! I wish you were there to protect me. I know you would've never let him do me the way that he did." She cried into my chest.

I was clenching my jaw so hard; I could taste this bitch ass nigga that was coming at my woman. He must have thought it was sweet or something. And why wouldn't he? After he had come into my home, tied me up, and had taken more then ten million dollars in heroin, I must have seemed more than sweet to his bitch ass. Yo, I felt like a straight sucka.

The worst feeling in the world for a man is when his woman has to run to him in fear after another man has defiled or violated her in some way. I was so heated that I was seeing stars. The high that I once had began to fade away quickly. I could feel Tori trembling against me and that had me vexed.

"Yo, chill, ma. I'ma take care of this nigga. Just give me a lil' time. For now, set up appointments with the Bloods women, and do their hair. We'll compensate our workers for doing so, don't worry about it. You hear me?

She nodded. "Yes. But I don't want you to do anything stupid. I need you. I love you, Showbiz."
I pulled her into a warm embrace and kissed her on

the forehead. "Yeah, I know, Ma. I gotta figure this shit out. I hate that you're in the middle, but you knew what it was when you started fucking wit' a nigga."

"Yeah, but its not just about us no more." She took a step back and rubbed her belly that protruded from her blouse. "We're pregnant, daddy. I hope you're happy about it." She looked up into my eyes in worry.

At that revelation, my high dissipated. I looked down at her stomach completely sober. I didn't know how I felt about her being pregnant. I wasn't happy. I wasn't sad. I think I was sicker, but only because I was broke. I didn't know what to say or do. So I just held my silence and hugged her. I had to get my hands on sore serious cash and fast.

I needed to get at least a few million so I could pay back Javier. Then I could hit the slums and start to come up on the bread that my father needed in order to hand me over his throne. I couldn't think when I was sober. I needed a fix. After I got my fix, I knew where my first stop would be. A stop that would guarantee me a few million, at least I hoped.

\* \* \*

It was hot and humid on a sunny afternoon. I could feel a slight breeze of the wind as it coursed through the open driver's side window in Tori's Benz truck that I'd bought her when she'd first crossed over to be with me.

I felt like scum having to drive my woman's whip because mine was out of commission for the moment. I had yet cop to something, but it was on my agenda before I had hit rock bottom. I stepped out of the truck on my way to Debra into the dry heat, which was my half brother, Tristian 's mother.

Debra was five feet five inches tall, caramel-skinned with brown eyes and shoulder length hair. She was a real estate mogul and one of the coldest business women I'd ever met in my entire life. She had her hand in nearly everything from restaurants to beauty supply stores, salons to car washes and even the stock market. She was a beast and all about the come up. There was only one thing that I disliked about her.

Her and my mother hated each other even though Debra looked at me like I was her biological son. She did ever since I was young when she and my father came to be. I had a lot of respect for her. But not only respect, sexual attraction too. Debra was gorgeous.

She was one of those older women that kept herself up. She went to the gym three times a week. She ate right and made sure she got adequate amounts of sleep. Her ways to me were all sensual and alluring. I personally ain't have no filter, so I was accustomed to letting her know what was on my mind. I also had a hard time keeping my hands to myself even though my dad had a habit of chastising me about it.

I didn't give a fuck about that or the fact she was once my father's wife and my brother's mother. Just wasn't important. I needed these funds and I knew she was the only one who could help.

I rang the doorbell a few times and waited for her to answer it. After what seemed like an eternity, her maid answered the door in her black and white uniform. She was an older Mexican lady I assumed or someone of Spanish descent like myself.

"I'm sorry. I was upstairs vacuuming. I didn't hear the doorbell until just now," she said in a cheerful voice. "Are you looking for Mrs. Vega?"

I nodded. Even though my father and Debra had been divorced, she'd held on to his last name for whatever reason. "Yeah, I'm saying, didn't they call you from the gate house before they let me through?" I asked irritated.

She smiled. "I was trying to finish up this last bit of work. It completely slipped my mind. I'm sorry."

I stepped inside into the big, marble looking living room. It was completely spotless. There was a fountain in the center, along with small statues. It was decked out with white leather couches, crystal chandeliers, thousand-dollar paintings, and gorgeous plants. Debra had impeccable taste.

"Where's she at?" I asked, looking around extremely jealous and irritable.

She stepped past me. "Follow me. She's right out here reading alongside the pool. She only got out a few minutes ago, so she shouldn't be too far into the book she's reading. She replied to me in Spanish. She seemed like she was in a great mood.

"Bitch! Shut the fuck up! I don't care about none of that shit. Just lead me to her. No need to use up all your word count, shit." I curled my lip and frowned my face.

I was in a horrible mood. The only thing that was on my mind was how Wetto had got down on Tori and her workers. Javier had been hitting my phone all night. I was low on product and on top of that, I felt like I was behind in the race for my father's throne. My mind wasn't right. The last thing I needed to hear was a bitch with a cheerful ass voice.

She sped up the pace, leading me to the backyard. "There she is, sir." She called to her. "Senora, you have a guest. Your son is here." She bowed her head and backed into the house.

I walked towards Debra, shielding my eyes from the sun. She was laid out in a lounge chair beside the pool with a sun hat on. The rays of the sun reflected off the clear blue waters of her long pool and her caramel skin. She was dressed in a two-piece bikini, the top barely covering her double D breasts. The bottom half of her bikini hugged her pussy. I could see that even from the distance I stood. I made my way over to her, feeling my penis swell in my pants.

"Mama, what it do? I see you out here enjoying this sun. Or should I say this sun is enjoying you?" I flirted.

She looked up from her book and lowered her blue Chanel sunglasses. She sat up on the chair before getting to her feet. "Hey there, baby. Long time no see. Come over here and give me my hug with yo' handsome self." She held out her arms for me.

I walked into them and held her close. Her perfume wafted up my nose, intoxicating me like crazy. I inhaled her and held her small frame in my arms. Everything about her was natural. No fake ass nor titties. All real. Nothing like the women in New York. Debra was from Chicago by way of Memphis. She was country fed and Chicago bred. She had the charm of a Southern Belle, and the jazziness of a sharp tongue from the land of the windy city.

I kissed her neck and ran my hands down her lower back, all the way down to her brown ass cheeks that were sliced down the middle by a baby blue thong. I cuffed her cheeks and sucked on her neck. She wiggled out of my grasp, pushing me away. "I told you about that. You're like a son to me. Tsk, Juanito." She wagged her finger at me.

I laughed, reaching down into my pants to readjust myself. Her beautiful nipples threatening to spill from her bikini top did little to help ease the pain of my throbbing dick.

She sat back in her lounge chair and crossed her thick thighs. "So, what brings you to my home unannounced? You must be in trouble." She picked up the glass of pink lemonade from the Umbrella table that was right next to her and sipped from it.

I grab one of the available lounge chairs and positioned it directly in front of her. I wanted the perfect view of her fat pussy while we talked. She was so fuckin' fine to me. I couldn't help but to lust. I had a thing for older women. I just never took the time to pursue them because it seemed like too much work. I didn't like broads who called themselves calling me out on my bullshit and older women had a way of doing that. My preference was submissive women. The ones who kept their mouths closed when told and allowed me to spoil them. I hated to be challenged.

"About a week ago, I got robbed, ma. Some nigga caught me slipping and hit me for ten million in heroin. I had all of my money tied up into that shipment. I'm fucked up right now. I need help and I'll do whatever it takes to get it."

She took another sip out of her pink lemonade and uncrossed her thighs, exposing exactly what was in my line of vision to see. "So, what do you want from me besides the obvious, of course?"

My dick was pulsating in my boxers. I wanted to pull it out and stroke it while I looked between her legs. I could cum just off the image of her. That's how beautiful she looked and how crazy I was over her.

"I need about three million and I should be able to pay you back in no more than a month, if that. I got some shit lined up, and as long as everything goes as planned, I can't lose.

She opened her legs wider and removed the glasses from her face, setting them on the table. She looked into my eyes. "How is your mother? I haven't seen her in a while. How did she take the news about Maine? I'm sorry to hear about that by the way." She pursed her lips and shook her head.

I shrugged. "She's okay. She took the news hard but is recovering just fine. She's a fighter, just like you. As hard as it may be to believe, y'all are alike in many ways."

Her eyes got big before they turned into slits. "Never say that to me again. Yes, my love for you is unconditional, but me and Amelia have history that is not so good. She feels like I stole your father away from her. I feel like he played us both, but life goes on. In order to survive in this world, a woman has to outthink every man around her and capitalize off them in any way she can.

A man is driven by his penis. A woman is driven by her ambitions. The next time you see her, tell her

I send my regards." She smiled. "As far as you go, you're my baby, Juanito. You know I can't turn you down. The three million is yours. You'll have a month to pay me back. I'll wire it to you within the next hour or so. I'll need your information."

A fly landed on her right thigh. She swung her hand and tried to smack it but missed. This act caused her to open her thighs wider. Her pussy swallowed the crotch band of her thong. Both lips were fully exposed and freshly shaven I could tell.

Something in me snapped. Before I could stop myself, my head was between her thighs. I opened them wider, licking at her exposed lips.

She bucked against me, shaking. "Aww, stop, Juanito. This ain't right." She opened her legs even more, yet tried to push me away.

I gripped her thighs, pulling her close to my mouth. I moved her panties to the side and slithered my tongue up and down her slit, tasting her.

"Un! Oooh, Juanito, stop. Stop. Please, shit!" she moaned as she closed her eyes.

I reached up and yanked her bra away. Her titties spilled out into the open with light stretch marks across them that made them look so real but sexy to me. Her dark brown areolas covered most of her breast.

I slid two fingers into her pussy, working them in and out. She wrapped her legs around my head and rode my face. "Aw! Aw! Ah! Fuck! Son! Ooh! Shit! I'm cumming! I'm cumming!" she moaned, biting into her bottom lip.

I waited until she rubbed her pussy all over my face, before I stood up and dropped my pants. My dick was killing me. "Debra, you gotta give me this shit. Please, I ain't gone say shit to your son. That's my word. I need this pussy. Come on." I lowered myself between her legs.

She shook her head and beat my chest. "No! Don't, Juanito! Your father gone kill us. I can't do this!" she hollered and tried to fight me off.

I allowed her to punch me all in the back. I wiggled my hips from right to until I found her hole with my dick head. I slammed it home.

"Uh, fuck! Baby, why?" She closed her eyes tight as I began to long stroke her pussy like a monster. "Uh. Uh. No. No. Baby. Uh. Fuck. Stop, Juanito. Stop. Uh, yes!"

The chair broke and we fell to the pavement with my dick going in and out of her womb like a battering ram. My mouth was all over her gorgeous breasts, pulling the nipples with my teeth. For a woman in her forties, her pussy was nice and tight. Wet and sticky. Her walls sucked at me and tried to keep me inside every time I tried to pull back.

I started to imagine all the times I saw her walking around in just her little skippy gowns when her and my father was together when I was just a kid. All of the see-through nightgowns and short robes. All of the times I caught her lounging by the pool like she was today. All of the dreams I'd had of her. I pushed her knees to her breasts and got to killing that shit.

"Baby. Baby. Ah, son. Fuck!" she screamed. "Aww, fuck! Don't cum in me! Don't cum in me! Please, Juanito!" She sucked her bottom lip into her mouth as her as rolled to the back of her head.

The maid ran out but stopped in her tracks with her hand over her mouth. "Ay, dios mio!"

"Kiss me, Debra! Un. Un. Kiss my fucking lips. Now!" I hollered, piping her down. Her juices were dripping from my balls. I could feel her walls vibrating and sucking at me.

I leaned forward and kissed her lips. I felt all the tingling shoot to the head of my dick. I slammed into her repeatedly until I came all over her belly, breasts, and pussy. I fell on top of her, breathing heavily.

She sat up and exhaled. "Yo' father gon' kill you if he ever finds out about this. Do you want that money in cash or wired?"

I was a street nigga, so of course I chose the cash.

## Chapter 7

I got the three million dollars in cash from her three days later at seven in the morning. She showed up at my house with two duffle bags, dropping them on the floor right in the living room. "Here you go, son. Go and get your paper right. The world can never respect a broke man. I know you ain't trying to be in the way, are you?"

I shook my head. "Hell n'all. You know better than that." She smiled.

"I want my money back in thirty days. Never burn a bridge that you'll need to travel back across. I place my faith in you. I'll see you soon." She stepped forward and kissed both of my cheeks and got ready to walk away. I grabbed her lil' ass to me and cuffed her ass that was encased inside of a Dolce and Gabbana black shirt. Brought my lips to her and tongued her ass down for a full two minutes. By the time I stepped back, we were both breathing hard.

"I got you, ma. I'll see you as soon as I get right. That's my word." She wiped her lips with her right thumb and made her way out of my crib. Her skirt was so tight that I could make out the roundness of her ass. It looked so good that I wanted to lick up and down it.

I closed the door behind her and peeked out of the window. Her driver opened the back door to her limo before she got inside of it. Seconds later, the stretch Navigator pulled away from the curb.

I turned around to see Tori standing in the dinning room with her hand on her with her eyebrow raised damn near to her hair line. "Damn, that bitch just came all into our crib and you tongued her ass down. I thought y'all was finna fuck right there on the carpet. What's all that about?" she asked, stepping into the living room. "I thought that was Tristian's mother."

"I don't give a fuck who mother it is. That bitch just dropped me off three million dollars. I'm about to hit the ground running. I got a trick for that nigga, Wetto. Watch this shit." She swallowed, as I knelt down and reached into the bag of money.

"That's cool and all baby, but I can't help but feel a little disrespected by what I just saw. I mean it was a whole 'nother ass woman in our crib sucking and kissing all over you. That's pissing me off." She balled her hands into fists.

"Tori, fall back lil' one. Like I said, that bitch just dropped me off three million dollars. If you got down like that, then I'd be kissing you instead and there would be no reason for me to put my tongue in her. I ain't trying to hear all that whiny shit right now. Take yo' ass in the room and let me do my thing out here. Word up. Go." I pointed to the back of the house. She shook her head.

"Fuck that, Showbiz! I'm feeling some type of way. I got your baby inside of me now and I deserve a little bit more respect then what you are accustomed to rendering unto me. I ain't some weak bitch. I just submit to you because I love your crazy ass. Now I ain't like what I just saw. Don't bring them bitches to our home. That's that!" she snapped.

I stood up and turned around to face her. "Who the fuck you think you talking too, bitch? This is my muthafucking house. I'll bring whoever I wanna bring up into this muthafucka. You being pregnant don't change shit. Fuck you thought this was?" She frowned and looked up at me.

"Nigga, I'm not scared of you. You think just because I keep my tongue to myself that I'm afraid. Nigga, please. I daddy this and daddy that because it's important that I play a role for your ego. Don't mistake the role I play in this movie you're starring in to be that of my real character because it ain't. Ain't nothing you can do to me that I can't do to you, nigga."

I swung and smacked her with my right so hard, she flew into the wall and bounced off of it. "Bitch! I'll kill you in this muthafucka. Don't you ever poke yo' chest out at me!"

She bounced off of the carpet and ran into my face, punching me in the nose and bussing my shit. Then she had the nerve to kick me in the nuts. "You ain't gon' put yo' hands on me and think I ain't gon' fight yo' ass back. I'm from Gary, Indiana. We get it in."

She started to attack me by swinging her arms wildly. Her fists bounced off my head and face, fucking me up. I stumbled backward with my nuts in my lower abs. I tried to catch my breath, but Tori kept coming like a maniac. I couldn't believe she had that much heart. It shocked the shit out of me.

I fell on my back and threw my guards up. I was waiting for my balls to drop again. They acted like they were on the run from her crazy ass. Jealousy was a muthafucka, I see. She straddled me and continued to rain down her fists.

"You not gon' do me like you did Punkin. I'll kill you first. I love you too much, Showbiz. I'm your baby mother now!" She slipped a punch through my guards and bussed me in the nose again. Blood gushed out of it right away. That was it. I humped and threw her off of me. Grabbed a handful of her hair and smacked her across the face five quick times.

"Bitch. You. Think. This. Shit. Is. A. Game?" I threw her ass to the carpet and got on top of her. Grabbing her by the throat and choking the shit out of her.

"Ack! Ack! Stop!" She kicked her legs wildly. Her eyes were wide open, turning redder and redder.

I laid my cheek against hers. "Bitch, don't you know I'll kill yo' punk ass, huh? You fucking wit' a monster. I'll leave you dead right here on this carpet if I didn't care about you and respect how you just came at me." I squeezed harder and harder, digging my nails into her skin and everything. I wanted that shit to hurt and bleed. I was hoping my nails left scars. I wanted her to remember how close she'd come to death fucking wit' me.

The kicking of her legs grew weaker and weaker, until they barely kicked at all. Her face turned bright red. Her eyes rolled into the back of her head before the lids of her eyes closed. I continued to choke her watching her strain in the face. I waited until she stopped moving before I sat back on my haunches.

I wiped the blood from my nose and put it on the white beater she wore on top of her white bikini cut panties. I looked down on her, breathing hard. I could make out her belly under her shirt. It looked like a small cantaloupe. Her arms were stretched out at her sides.

I hollered into her face. "You see what happens when you fuck wit 'a nigga like me. Bitch. I can take yo' life whenever I want to. You're lucky to be alive. I don't need you, you need me." I rocked back and forth, as the blood dripped out of my nostrils.

Her face was starting to turn blue and swell up. I got to thinking about how good of a woman she was. How she'd gone against her whole family for me. She took great care of Maine when he was alive, making sure I stayed in his life despite the naggin' from Ebony. She was always kind and supportive of me. I knew without a shadow of a doubt that she had my back against all odds and that she loved me unconditionally.

Maybe I had been bogus for letting Debra step into her home and put her lips on me. I should have had more respect for a woman like Tori. I saw that now. Even through my addiction, she had stood by me and held me down. Shit was getting real in the streets for me. I needed her. She was the only real love I had outside of my mother. I started to do CPR on her right away, blowing into her mouth and giving her chest compressions.

"One, two, three, four."

I blew into her mouth again and watched her chest heave upward, before descending. Suddenly, I didn't want her to die. I needed her to stay alive. I needed her by my side. I wished I hadn't gone so over board. I cursed my horrendous temper. I applied more chest compressions.

"Come on Tori, baby. Don't die! Daddy need you, lil' mama."

I pinched her nose and blew into her mouth again, before following the same routine of CPR. I'd taken the course one summer when I was fourteen-years old when my father sent me and my brothers off to the Boy Scouts of America. I remembered back then thinking that learning that technique was dumb and a waste of time.

I wanted to go swimming, play basketball, or on a scavenger hunts in the woods. I didn't like the counselors made us pair off in the gym to take the CPR class. But now I was thankful for it. I blew into her mouth for the sixth time and surrendered so much air into her that I grew light-headed.

She jerked two times, then started to cough harshly. "Uh-a! Uh-a! Uh-a!" She hacked a loogey and spit it on the carpet, before rolling to her side and coughing even harder. "You son of a bitch! You could have killed me!" She hacked, holding her throat.

I knelt down and forced her into my embrace, holding her as tight as I could. "Baby, I'm sorry. I swear to God I am. I love you so fucking much. I'll never do that again. I promise." I rocked back and forth with her, feeling the tears sting my eyes. I was going to try as hard as I could to never take our fights to that level of abuse again. I had almost lost her and I never wanted to do that.

She cried in my arms. "Showbiz, you ever do that shit to me again, I'm gon' find a way to kill you. On everything I love. I'm gon' take your life. Just love me, damn, without all that extra bullshit! Is that so hard?" she cried.

"Nah, ma, it ain't. I'ma do my best, bae. You hear me? I know you got my shorty in there. I was bogus and I know it."

\*\*\*

Later that same night, I took one million dollars of the cash that I'd gotten from Debra and sat it in front of Veeto. We were at his crib out in West Queens, New York. There was a bottle of Patron on top of the table along side of the money and two ounces of heroin. He sat across from me with his eyes low and powder residue on his upper lip. He nodded in and out, then pulled on his nose. His attic felt stuffy and almost swamp-like.

"Yo son, that's a million dollars right there kid. For that million I ain't gon' have no other choice other than to give you the Savage Package." He separated another line of heroin, and got it ready to be tooted.

I was already fucked up. I'd shot two grams of Vega heroin into my veins before I'd arrived at his crib. I was lifted and feelin' like killing somethin'. "Yo, what is the Savage Package, kid?" He finished the line and sat back in his seat after grabbing the bottle of Patron.

"Nigga, I know you're a lil' turnt off by Bloods right now, but don't let that perturb you from the ones out here in Queens. Especially not the ones that run under me. We're a different tribe with different values and beliefs. Them Harlem niggas are foul anyway. You should have known that. I mean no disrespect to you and all, but that Savage Package gets you two of my hit squads. Niggas I've assembled that are about that life on every level when it comes to this murder shit. Real Bloods that love seeing nigga's bleed. Nah' mean?"

He took a long swallow of the drank. "In addition to the savages, I'ma load you up with as much weaponry as you need to take care of your business. I got the low down on that fuck nigga Wetto's people. As crazy as it may sound, one of my baby mother's is cousin to his main bitch. But I don't fuck wit her people like that, so I don't care what happens to her.

The nigga ducked off out there in Manhattan. He got a nice lil' crib. You know how niggas do. They stay out in the burbs, but come back to their stomping grounds to fuck the community up. Me and the nigga on smooth terms. He just hit my phone about three hours ago asking me if I wanted to try some of his new work. This the shit I'm tooting right now. Had I known it was the shit he'd hit you for, I would have never indulged. But it's too late now." He sat back in his chair and closed his eyes.

"How many niggas in each squad?" I asked, grabbing the bottle of Patron and drinking out of it. I needed to know what I was getting for my money.

"Eight niggas in each squad. Sixteen altogether. All would be taking orders straight from you because they are loyal to me and I'm the one that feed their families. You dig me? You'll have full control of them for three months. That means that anything you say goes."

That's how it works out in New York. There was always some major nigga calling shots from a far that was the head of groups of killers. I didn't give a fuck if you were red or blue, or one of the deadly Spanish gangs, if you were plugged, you ran under some nigga who called the shots over you.

And when it came down to the nitty gritty, you had a nigga like me that came along that was able to rent killers to follow my every command. I had never been apart of the equation before, but due to the fact that I was a Blood nigga, I could have been. I needed these dudes. I had a bunch of business to handle and I couldn't handle none of that shit without a bunch of certified head bussers around me.

"Yo, I'ma fuck wit' you. Make sure you align me with straight lunatics that's gon' listen and pay attention. You handle that and we got a deal. Huh?" I pushed the bag of money across the table at him.

He grabbed it, and set it on the floor. "I got mad love for you kid. On behalf of my Bloods, I just wanna say that was some bullshit that Wetto pulled, so whatever you about to do to that fool, he got it coming. It is what it is." He tooted another line of heroin and frowned his face.

"When I get through with this nigga won't nobody ever cross the Vegas again. You can bank on that statement." I had visions of murdering Wetto's whole family in cold blood. I wanted to torture his punk ass before I killed him. He'd betrayed me in the worst way and then took it upon himself to go at my lady. That meant that all family members were fair game. That shit was right up my alley. I couldn't wait to get down on him. "Yo, I'm looking for my three months to start first thing in the morning. I'll be in touch."

\*\*\*

When I stepped out of Veeto's crib, it was pouring rain with huge lightning bolts flashing across the sky. The rain was coming down so hard that it felt like hail. I rushed out into it and got into my whip. Fifteen minutes later and with a bottle of Patron in my hand, I was back sitting on Eve's grave. The soil had turned into mud. Thunder roared loudly as I sat facing her tombstone. I ran my fingers across the part of the grave that said born 1997 and died 2018. I still couldn't believe that she was gone. I squeezed my eyelids and allowed for the tears to drop out of them.

"I miss you so fucking much, Eve. Why did you have to go, ma? I hollered as lightning flashed across the sky and the thunder boomed somewhere close by.

The rain crashed into the land all around me loudly. I could smell wet grass and dirt. The air tasted salty. I swallowed and laid my head against the headstone. I couldn't stop the tears from coming. I felt so weak and emotional. Once again, the childhood that I'd shared with Eve ran through my mind. I saw us in the hallways in high school hugged up, me walking her to her locker possessively. Even when I had my arm around her, multiple girls at school still tried to get at me as if she weren't even standing there. That only happened a few times before Eve started to check hoes and shortly thereafter, whooping their asses over me.

After getting suspended more times than I could remember, she'd finally came to the conclusion that we would be better off as friends because I was a straight sex-crazed whore. I agreed even though I remembered feeling crushed back then. I'd never gotten the chance to tell her how I really felt about her decision. I think I had hurt her so bad that she'd turned to women. I didn't know for sure if that was the reason why, but I had never asked. All I knew is that I was missing her like crazy.

All of my clothes were soaked. It felt like they weighed at least five pounds now. I looked at her name on the tombstone. "Eve, I love you, baby. I wish I had stopped you from taking your life. I wish I would have known, Queen, but I was stupid. I didn't know what you were really going through. I should have listened. Should have remembered that even though you were my right hand man that you were also a female, that you needed me emotionally. I was selfish, bae. I swear to God I was so fucking selfish."

I cried my heart out, shaking my head. My knees slouched through the mud as I turned to place my back against her tombstone. I pulled my syringe out of my inside coat pocket, then brought my arm out of it, as well. I smacked my arm a few times, before pricking the needle into the thick vein on the inside of my forearm, and injecting the heroin into my system.

The drug entered into my blood stream and caused my body to shake in bliss. Eve's face popped inside of my mind. She was smiling and shaking her head at the same time. I licked my lips and closed my eyes. I felt closer to her. Closer to the only best friend that I had ever known. I felt that she lived deep down inside of me.

"Eve, I'm coming to be with you, ma. I ain't gon' be down here much longer. It's too much shit going on and it's getting hectic. Muthafuckas gotta pay, baby. These muthafuckas gotta pay for what they did to me and then I'm coming home to you, ma. Word is bond." I laid against her headstone with my eyes closed. The rain pelted my face. I drifted away into a deep sunken place. I needed an escape. I was tired of life.

# Chapter 8

"A'ight, then my nigga, Showbiz. He ain't just my nigga, this my muthafucking kinfolk right here, kids. I want you muthafuckas to roll behind my dude and follow his every command. It's a lot of shit that's about to go down and each one of you were hand-picked for the mission, coming highly recommended by me. Don't make me look like a fucking fool. If that happens, the punishment is death for you and your entire household. That's on my blood. With that being said, my nigga wanna say a few words, so listen the fuck up." Veeto's voice boomed throughout the cloistered basement of his crib out in Queens.

I scratched my inner arm where I was accustomed to putting my needle. For some reason, it was itching me like crazy. "Yo, I'm on some no mercy, no remorse type of shit. You niggas need to follow me and listen up closely because for the next three months, we're going to be bound at the hip. I got love for Veeto and I can't see him steering me wrong. Each and every last one of you were specifically picked for the type of shit that I got in mind."

I looked around at the soldiers. They had red rags around their necks. Some of them had them covering half of their faces. The ones whose faces I could see were turned into an angry snarl. They nodded as I spoke. I could feel the presence of killers all around me and I loved it. I was ready to get the show on the road.

Veeto stood up and started to shake it up with the two hit squads of killers. "Yo, I got mad love for each and every last one of you niggas. While you're at war with the homey, just know that I'm here for you and I got your families. Handle that bitness and stand on that rag. Suuwoo!"

The hit squads began to chant "Suuwoo" as loud as they could until they were jumping up and down in place all geeked up. I could feel the heroin rushing through my veins. I felt amped up, as well. I nodded my head and closed my eyes for a second, visualizing Eve's face. I missed her so fucking much. And while I was doing my thing, I knew she'd be looking down on me with a mug on her face.

Veeto came over and put his arm around my neck. "Yo, kid, make sure you keep me updated with everything you're doing. I'll also need progress reports on my soldiers. If anyone of these niggas ain't acting right or handling their bitness like they'tr suppose to be, you let me know and I'll take care of them right away. I'm here for you, son. Make sure you know that what I'm doing is bigger than the money." He grabbed me and gave me a brief hug.

I shook my head. "If a muthafucka ain't following my orders, I'll handle them myself. Ain't no snitch in me, Blood. I got this. Everybody gon' have their direct orders ahead of time. That's the best I can do. Disregard them orders and it's a wrap. Word is bond." I shook up with him.

He nodded and ran his tongue across his teeth. "Yeah, a'ight. But don't be on no lunatic type shit with my niggas, Blood. I know how you and my lil' niece Eve got down. Y'all love killing for the sport." He laughed and wiped his nose. "But every last one of these niggas know what they signed up for, so it is what it is. I'ma give you some more information that

I found on Wisin and Chulo and everything I got on Wetto so you can annihilate these niggas as soon as possible."

\*\*\*

I watched Tori slam another outfit into her suitcase with a mug on her face. She looked over at me and rolled her eyes. "Can you tell me why the fuck I gotta go to stay in a hotel in Jersey? Shut down all of my businesses for, what did you say, three weeks?" she asked.

I stood in the doorway trying to keep my cool, but once again, Tori was testing my patience. I exhaled and flared my nostrils.

"Yo, you doing what the fuck I'm telling you to do because I said so. I can't have you in the city right now. I'm about to go at this nigga Wetto for what he's done to us. You already knew I wasn't about to let that shit slide. And because I love and care about you so much, I need to know that you are safe and sound. That's just that. Now hurry the fuck up so I can get you across the bridge before midnight.

She shook her head and slammed a pair of pants into her Gucci luggage. "You know I really don't like the way you talk to me, Showbiz. You be coming at me like I'm one of them project hoes or something. I've stood by your ass for a minute now and I'm pregnant with your seed. You gotta start to respect me. I'm suppose to be your Queen. Straight up." She sighed and opened the door to her closet wider, yanking clothes off of the hangers.

"We about to lose all of this fucking money. Then if there is a war, who's to say that they won't burn my shops down to the ground? Wetto is one of those dirty ass Bloods. And every nigga and bitch that follows behind him is just as dirty. I mean I hope you kill his punk ass, but then again, I would be crazy if something happened to you. I mean I love you so fucking much that I hate it."

She stopped on her path to her luggage and placed a hand on her stomach. She closed her eyes and took five consecutive, deep breaths. Her jaws filled up with air before she blew it out.I pulled her to me and wrapped her into my arms. I could feel her tense up as if she wanted to push me away. I held her a bit tighter.

"Baby, I'm sorry. I have to do a better job with how I be coming at you because you are my Queen and I do respect you. You're the only one out here holding me down and I honor you for that, so forgive how I be coming at you. You know that old habits die hard. Now far as the businesses go, don't worry about the losses we'll take. We have to get rid of this nigga because he is like a plague.

As long as he has breath in his lungs, he's going to look to cause us a bunch of problems that will effect our income and it'll keep our safety in jeopardy. I can't allow that. My first priority is to make sure that you and our unborn child are safe and sound. Then secondly, that we protect our home front and keep our money flowing in by the bundles. As long as this fuck boy is alive, that ain't no guarantee, so I gotta do what I gotta. When it's all said and done, we'll be good. You have my word on that." I kissed her on the forehead.

"Okay, daddy. Well I'ma follow you and allow you to handle your business. I mean it's my place to do so. But please be careful and get this over with. Make sure you answer texts because I'm going to be so worried about you all the time." She wrapped her arms around me and laid the side of her face on my chest. "Daddy, it's only eight o'clock right now. Can we just chill for a few hours? Maybe order a pizza or something. I just want to spend a little time with you before you enter into this serious war. Is that so wrong?" She looked up at me with her big brown eyes.

For some reason, that question and the way she looked at me caused me to soften a little bit. I understood that Tori really cared about me. I think underneath the surface, she was scared for my well-being. She was, after all, carrying my child and a long way from her home in Gary, Indiana. I was all that she really had out in New York, so if anything happened to me, it would surely change her life for the worst.

I could also see the strangle marks around her neck from where I choked her out. I felt guilty about that. Wish I had never done it. She was such a good woman. I brushed her curly hair out of her face and kissed her lips. "Yeah, ma. We can take a few hours and just chill. Gon' head and order a pizza and I'ma go and get myself right. I'll meet you in the front room. I'ma let you pick the movie and everything."

She shook her head. "I don't want to watch a movie. I wanna pick your brain. I've never gotten the chance to actually sit down and listen to you speak. I have a few questions that I want to ask you, questions that God forbid if anything happened to you and you're not able to make it back to me, our child would at least like to know these things. And so would I, because you are a mystery and when it comes to me, you shouldn't be. So I'm going to order a nice Meat Lover's pizza, get out a carton of orange juice and we're going to sit on the carpet and talk for a little while. Then you can take me out to Jersey. How does that sound?"

My only response was to laugh and nod my head. The pizza arrived thirty minutes later and we were all set up in the living room ten minutes after that. Tori grabbed a slice and took a big bite out of it. The pizza sauce oozed over her fingers and a big sausage fell on to the box, along with a chunk of ground beef. She took a napkin and dabbed at the corners of her mouth.

"Um, now that's what you call a pizza." I nodded for a full minute, then snapped out of it and picked up a slice, biting into it. I was high as a kite. My eyes were low and threatening to close up on me. My veins tingled and I felt numb all over.

I licked my lips and looked over at her. I could see directly down her tank top. Both of her pretty titties looked as if they were glistening. " Tori, you so fucking bad. You know that?" I tried to open my eyes some more but it was a heavy task.

She smiled, took another bite, and chewed it, looking into my eyes. We were in the living room with a Jhene Aiko track playing softly out of the speakers. The lights were dimmed. We had a nice white and black tablecloth over the carpet where the box of pizza and Welch's orange juice was set up along with a nice amount of napkins. Tori wiped her mouth and took a swallow from her glass of juice.

"Okay, daddy. My first question for you is besides a dope boy, what do you want to be in life? Like when you finally decide to leave the game alone?" She bit into her pizza again.

I shrugged my shoulders. "Baby, I don't really know. Growing up, all I've ever wanted to be life was my father. In my opinion, he was a supreme hustler. I remember seeing him at the kitchen table chopping chunks off of kilos of dope. He'd have a pile of crack on one side of the table and on the other, there would be bundles of cash. I used to be mad that I had to go to school because my father told me when I was only five years old that he'd never finished school. But when he told me this, I remember him having two fists full of hundreds.

I'd never understood why a person had to finish school if they could have all of that money, so I never wanted to. I hated school. It made me feel dumb when other kids got something that I didn't. So, my whole life, all I've ever wanted to be like was my father. A dope boy turned King Pin with a bunch of loyal soldiers following behind me.

Tori smiled. "So even now, do you still feel the same way or have you evolved into wanting something greater than the dope game?"

I picked up my pizza again. "I just want to be rich and maybe run a few strip clubs. I haven't thought past the ghetto spectrum of things. I think maybe once I knock this nigga off, my mind will open up a little bit. But for now, I can't look that far into the future.

"What made you turn to heroin baby? I don't think you was doing that shit when Punkin was alive or maybe you were. I didn't watch you that closely. But what made you start doing this?"

She grabbed my arm and pointed at the prick marks along my inner forearm where I injected myself. I yanked my arm away.

"Damn, ma. What you got me on trial or some shit?" I snapped, looking her over distastefully.

"Baby, I didn't mean it like that. You know I'm going to be here for you no matter what. I'm just curious is all. I've always wanted to ask you that. So please tell me. I need to know."

I shrugged my shoulders again and sighed. "When I was growing up, that's all niggas did in Harlem was tooted Percocets and Oxycodones. All of the older niggas snorted that Boy because they had the money to do so, while us teens resorted to stealing pills out of our parent's medicine cabinets and shit like that. Every now and then, somebody would come up on a little heroin, but it was rare.

Anyway, when I got my money half way decent, I got me about a gram of it and I haven't looked back since then. I didn't start shooting this shit until this fuck nigga Wetto bussed this move on me. With the death of Eve, and then me losing Maine, plus ten million dollars in work, it just became way too much. I needed an escape and heroin has been my flight off of this island of pain. I wish I would have never started, but it's too late to cry over spilled milk."

I blew air out of my jaws. "Are we done now?" I asked, feeling some type of was. I was starting to feel too vulnerable. I didn't like that feeling. Especially in a matter of hours, I was about to be on kill mode. I didn't feel like being in a sappy or depressed mood. Luckily, I was high as fuck and it didn't really break through any of my emotional walls.

"Not yet. I got a few more questions, but none more important to me than the one I'm going to ask you first. You know, I'll just ask both and you can answer them in any order that you choose. I need your one hundred percent brutal honesty though. Please, daddy." She reached and laid her hand on my arm.

"A'ight, I'm giving you two more questions and then this interview is over. So make them your best ones. A'ight?"

She placed her small hand inside of mine and squeezed my fingers. "Okay, daddy. Here it goes." She took a deep breath. "Did you ever really love my sister? And what made you pursue me and turn me into your woman shortly after she died? I've always wanted to know this."

I shook my head. "To be honest, nah. I never loved her like that. I had love for her, but my nose wasn't wide open or anything. When I first started hussling, I noticed that all of the real major niggas had a woman at home that kept the house and held shit down on that front. Your sister was fine and a freak like I needed her to be. So I made her my in-house pussy. I don't know how things progressed past that.

Well maybe after I found out that she was pregnant with Maine, but I don't know. Me and your sister always butted heads. It didn't take much for us to get at each other's throat. With all of that arguing and bickering, it's real hard to fall into something emotional with a woman, so I never got the chance. Me and her were polar opposites. All we had in common was sex."

Tori dropped her pizza and wiped her mouth. "Wait a minute, Showbiz, because now you're getting me a little afraid. You've called me your in-house pussy a few times. All you and I do is argue and you've never told me you loved me until you found out that I was pregnant with our child. Why shouldn't I believe that you don't feel the same way about me that you did her?"

I laughed and pulled at the stray hairs on my chin. "Damn, I guess that does sound a lil' similar, huh?"

"Yeah, it does, and to be honest with you, it's freaking me out." She wiped her hands and stood up. " I wish I would have never asked you that last question because now I'm feeling some type of way."

I stood up and blocked her path from leaving the room. The Jhene Aiko track switched to a new song. I wrapped my arms around her lower waist.

"Baby, I have never loved your sister. No matter what we were going through, I've never told her that I loved her either. I just can't lie about something like that. My heart is very cold for the part. There is room for only a selective few in there and you are one of those people. You come right after my mother. I love you because you are an amazing woman.

I can tell that you really care for me. And that you will do all that you can to support me even throughout my struggles. On top of that, you were great to Maine, you saved my life, and you got mad heart. I still can't believe that you bussed my shit, but I love you for doing it." I smiled.

"So what made you pursue me? Because you couldn't have known what type of woman that I was. What made you go out on a limb and go after your son's mother's sister? Because that's not normal. I need to know this because I don't want to be some pawn in your game of life, Showbiz. Please be honest with me."

I sighed. "Well, pure attraction was the first thing. I always peeped how fucking fine you were. That you were soft-spoken, maybe even a little shy around me. Even though you saw how destructive your sister and I's relationship was, that didn't stop you from making sure that Maine stayed in my life or you from reaching out to me and keeping me in tune with his well-being.

I took that to mean that you had your own mind. That was attractive to me. Then the day you came over and told me that you had to travel by bus and train, I felt sick to my stomach. I couldn't believe that a female as cold as you had to travel like that. I wanted to upgrade you right away and snatch you off of the market. I wanted to make you my in-house pussy. But somewhere along the way, you became a female that I actually love and care for. I mean I can't explain it, but that's what it is."

She was quiet for a short time, then she looked up at me. "I can't really figure out right now but I love you, Showbiz. I hope that I really have a sincere place in your life because you live in my heart. I know you have to go back out to those streets. So when you go, I need you to know that I love you and

I'll be waiting on you whenever you get home." She stepped on her tippy toes and kissed my lips. "Oh, and if ever I detect that I am nothing more than what my sister was to you, Showbiz, I promise you on my unborn child, I will take you out the game. I mean that." She smiled, held the side of my face, then walked off and sat back in front of the box of pizza.

I laughed to myself. I ain't think for one second that she was serious about last part. She was pregnant and had a lot of emotional shit going on with her. I chopped her threats up to hormones and didn't take them seriously. I'd only met one female killer before in my life and that was Eve. Tori couldn't possibly have that G-shit in her.

# Chapter 9

While I'd been the plug for Wetto, he'd been the plug for his cousin, Kam. Kam was a major nigga on the black side of Harlem. Like us, he was a Blood nigga. I'd never met him face to face. I'd only heard about hit through Wetto. However, part of the information that Veeto had given me in regards to Wetto circled around Kam. He said that if I was looking to knock off and annihilate Wetto, it'd be smart for me to slump his cousin Kam as well, because even though they were on two different parts of Harlem, they ran it as one unit. He'd also heard that Wetto had given Kam half of the dope he'd robbed me for. It was all I needed to hear to get vexed. I made up my mind as soon as he gave me that information that both of them had to die.

Kam owned a furniture store on West One Fifty Third and Seventh Avenue. He was one of those hustlers that was trying to venture out into legit businesses. He had a few establishments all over Harlem and the Bronx. But I was told by Veeto that when it came down to him doing his books, he spent the most time at his furniture store out in Harlem. That's where I'd able to catch his ass slipping.

It was eleven o'clock at night on a Thursday. It was nice and breezy with a full moon in the sky. I sat back in the Jeep Grand Cherokee and watched as four niggas from my hit squad hid on the side of the back entrance. That's what Kam used as his only exit from his store after he'd locked it down for the night. They'd been waiting for about ten minutes when the back door opened and they rushed inside of it with pistols out. I saw flashes from their guns going off but heard no sounds. All of our weapons had silencers on them courtesy of the homey, Veeto.

I slid my mask all the way down my face and waited for the signal. I was still high from the two grams of heroin I'd shot into my system only ten minutes prior. I felt hot and my nose was stopped up. One of the hittas came out of the back door and waved me over. I cocked my nine millimeter and put it into the small of my back before jumping out of the truck and jogging passed Kam's Rolls Royce that was in the drive way. It was all red with the black guts. The grass felt crunchy under my Timbs. I rushed inside where one of my hittas stood in the doorway until I passed by him. Then he closed the door and locked it.

The first thing I noticed when I got inside was that they had Kam on his knees with a two Machs at the back of his head. All around the store were bodies from Kam's crew. They laid on the carpet twisted with blood leaking out of them. Three of them in all. I stepped in front of him and pulled my mask over my head. As soon as I did, he closed his eyes tight. I upped the nine millimeter and pointed it into his face.

"Bitch ass nigga, open yo eyes!" I demanded.

"N'all, son. Fuck that. Long as I don't see your face, so you ain't got no reason to kill me. I know somebody put you on to me. If it's about the money, I got three million in the safe in my office right now. You can have that and gon' on about yo' bitness." He swallowed and squeezed his eyes tighter. I fixed the hammer on my pistol, before smacking him as hard as I could across the face with it. I could feel the steel connect with his bone.

"Aw!" His skin tore and bled. He fell on to his side and kept his eyes closed. "What the fuck, man? I told you where the money is and how much. You ain't got no reason to fuck me up. Take that shit and go. I got a whole ass family!" he hollered.

"Pick his bitch ass up and hold him steady," I ordered my hittas.

"Nigga, that three million is chump change. If you got three million in your office, that mean you got more someplace else. Now I'm the nigga that Wetto's bitch ass ripped off for all of that dope. Word on the street is that he gave you some of my shit which makes you my enemy. You can either give me back my dope or come up with ten million dollars in cash. Have it your way. What's it gon' be?" I smacked him across the mouth with the butt of my gun. It crashed into his teeth and bent one of them inward. Blood appeared all around his gums.

His head jerked backwards. "Yo, I ain't have nothing to do with that. I don't fuck with Spanish Harlem, son. Whoever my cousin knocked off, that lick was on him. I paid him cash money for the product he gave me. It's been that way for almost a year now. He copped the dope and I'd buy it from him. You're barking up the wrong tree, son. Word is bond." Blood seeped out of his mouth, dripping over his lips and onto his chest.

"Say, Blood. I said you can either come up with ten million dollars in cash or give me back my dope. Which is it gon' to be? I ain't got all fucking day." I grabbed him by his throat.

"Say something, fuck nigga."

"All I got is five altogether and about ten birds left. You can have that shit, just leave me with my life. This shit ain't worth my life, man. I just had my first son. He ain't even three weeks old." He ran his tongue across his swollen lips and swallowed the blood.

"If you got three million in your office here, where is the other two?" No matter what, five million dollars was half way to ten. I needed that lil' cash. It would make up for the ten that I'd lost fucking with Wetto's ratchet ass. There was also the fifteen million that my father needed in order to launch the Senator's campaign. I was thinking that if I could get the five million from Kam and take the ten birds and flip them, I could get closer to the amount needed.

"I got the other two at my crib out in the Bronx. It's in the kitchen behind the refrigerator. My baby mother know the code to my safe. I can have her pop it, take the bread, and bring it here. It ain't no thang, homey. Just leave us with our lives. I don't give a fuck what you do to Wetto. If you don't kill him, I will because this some bullshit. I don't fuck with Spanish Harlem. Never have, never will."

I started to search this nigga until I found his cell phone. "What's this bitch number?" I asked, looking him over.

"She's already in my call log. Just scroll down until you see the name Lady. Click on that and when she pick up, put the phone to my ear." A thick rope of blood dripped from the broken tooth in his mouth.

*Bam!*

I kneed him as hard as I could right in his shit, causing him to spit the tooth across the room. "I'm tired of you acting like you running shit. Shut the fuck up and let me run this bitch. You hear me?"

He frowned as more blood poured out of his mouth. One of his eyes was turning purple from when I'd smacked him across the face. "I got you, boss. Let's get this shit over with." He continued to keep his eyes closed. I dialed Lady's number. It rang three times before she picked up with a cheerful voice.

"Bae, what's taking you so long? Your food over here getting cold as hell?"

I flipped it to speakerphone and placed it beside Kam's bleeding face. "She say yo' food getting cold, my nigga. We better hurry this process along." I laughed.

"Hello, who is this? Somebody playing on the phone?" Lady asked. Kam spit blood on the carpet again. " N'all, bae. It's me and get that bread for me. I'll be there to pick it up in a minute."

" Kamron, baby. Are you okay? What's going on?" she asked in a strained voice.

"Yo, don't even worry about it. Just do like I say. I need you to clean that bitch out and have it by the front door. My mans gon' come and get it. The quicker he get that, the faster I'll be able to come from up under this." He hawked and spit a bloody loogey on to the floor.

"Baby, I'm scared. I think I'm finna call the police."

"Yo, you better tell that bitch what's gon' happen if she do that. My word, that's gon' be a fucked up situation."

"Don't do that, ma. Just do what I'm telling you to do because if you don't, they're going to waste our family. It's just money, baby. I'll get it again. Go and get that bread. Don't call nobody. Don't stress yourself. Just handle that business and we'll be okay. I promise you. Do you hear me?"

I could hear her crying. "Yes, I hear you. I'm going to do it right now. Please don't hurt my man whoever you are. I'll have the money ready for you when you get here. I swear!"

"We'll be there in about ten minutes. Have it by the door. And you stay on this phone until they get there. Matter fact, what's your favorite song because I want you to sing it to me while you're taking care of this business."

"I don't have a favorite song," she cried. " I just want my man home," she cried.
"Bitch, you better find one. Now pick one and sing it to me!" She whimpered before I heard her take a deep breath. *"You're the man. Baby, I adore. I gave you everything. What's mine is yours. I want you to live your life of course. But I hope you get what you're dying for. Be careful wit' me. Do you know what you're doing? Whose feelings that you're hurting and—*Why am I singing right now. It doesn't make sense?" she screamed.

"Bitch, shut up and keep singing and get that money together." She continued to sing the Cardi B. track. I could hear her take breaks to sniffle,.

I muted the phone. "Bitch nigga, give me the address so I can have my mans go and snatch that lil' paper up. Hurry up!" He hollered out the address before his head dropped to his chest with his eyes still closed tightly.

I got it and gave it to the leader of the first hit squad. His name was Blackie. He was about two hundred and fifty pounds, dark-skinned with a big stomach and short dreads. "Blood, take this information and go and snatch that lil' package up. Hit my phone as soon as you get there. I'ma hit yo' hand quite handsomely for this. Now go. Take two of your hittas wit' you."

" A'ight, Blood. This about a half hour away. I'll hit you in a minute. I watched him tap two of his guys on their shoulders and directed them to follow him out the back door which they did.

"Y'all pick his bitch ass up and bring him in the back to his office so he can open this safe. Let's go, muthafucka." I smacked him across the face again and wiped my bloody glove on his shirt. I could hear his bitch singing the "Be Careful" song in the background.

They picked him up and we made our way through the dark store until we got into his office where I flipped the switch. " A'ight, nigga. Where the fuck this safe at?"

"It's behind the filing cabinet, closer to the carpet. Just move it out the way. Man, once y'all get all of this bread and dope, just go, man. My beef ain't gon' be with you niggas. I know how the game go. This drama was brought to me because of the company I kept. I'ma go at Wetto now, you niggas. That's on my Blood."

"Move that filing cabinet. Hurry up," I ordered the two hittas that were holding Kam. They released him and did as they were told. They scraped the metal filing cabinet across the floor. Once it was moved, one of them knelt down and pulled a string that was sticking out of the wall. A panel on the wall flipped outward, exposing a five-foot safe with a digital face on it.

"Yo, it's gon' need a hand print. Once I put it on there I'ma punch in my ten digit code and it'll open. That's all there is to it." He wiped some blood from his mouth.

" A'ight then." I grabbed him by the back of the neck and threw him in front of the safe. Do what you gotta do, nigga. But hurry the fuck up!" I could hear his girl on the phone. She started the song from the top and began to sing it all over again. Kam crawled to the safe and felt around blindly with his eyes closed. He placed his hand on everything but the fucking safe.

"Nigga, open your fucking eyes so you can see what you're doing."

"N'all, son. I ain't trying to identify you, then you'll have to kill me. I'm Harlem, nigga. I know how this shit go. Long as I don't see your face, you ain't got no reason to put one in my dome." He continued to feel around for the safe.

I grabbed the back of his head and slammed it into the wall over and over again. "Bitch. Ass. Nigga. Didn't. I. Tell. You. That. You. Ain't. Running.

Shit!" I hollered, splattering his blood all over the room.

My hittas took a step back and bucked their eyes wide.

"Okay! Okay! Okay! Stop, nigga. Damn!" he hollered before falling on his ass with his face swelling up like a pumpkin. He hurried to his knees and rushed to his safe. He opened the panel flap where his hand was supposed to go, placing his right hand over it. It scanned it up and down in red, before turning green.

*"Please enter your ten digit code,"* the machine chimed. With blood dripping from his face and his left eye closing, Kam entered the ten-digit code and sat back on his haunches.

"I'ma kill that nigga Wetto, Dunn. Word to my mother." The safe popped open, he pulled the door wide for me to see all of the money and dope on the inside. "There you go, Money. We should be fair and square." I noticed his girl stopped singing on the phone.

"Baby, somebody knocking on the door," she whimpered. My phone vibrated with a text from Blackie It simply read: *Touchdown.*

I flipped the phone off of mute. "Shorty, go and answer the door. That's my mans and nem right there. You got the money ready?"

"Yes, I got it right in the hallway by the front door. I just want to hand it out to them. I don't want them coming inside of my house. I got kids in here," she cried.

"A'ight, let me tell 'em what it do." I muted her and sent Blackie a text saying. *Get everything and finish the whole crib.*

"A'ight, shorty. I just told him what it was. Gon' head and open the door."

"Okay." There was silence and then I could hear her talking.

"Here go all of the money right here. Your boss said that there is no reason for you to—Ah! Oh my God! What are you doing?"

"Shut up bitch!" came Blackie's voice.

"A, man. I thought if you got the money that you was gon'—."

I aimed and fired two shots into the back of his head. I watched him jerk violently on his shoulders, before falling forward into a pool of his own blood. I cleared out the safe and forced his body inside of it, before closing it back and placing the filing cabinet in front of it.

## Chapter 10

Kalani woke me up the next morning beating on my door like she'd lost her fucking mind. I damn near had a heart attack jumping out of the bed. I thought she was the police or one of my enemies. It didn't dawn on me that an enemy would more than likely never beat on your front door because they wanted to catch you off guard. So I jumped out of the bed and grabbed two .45 with silencers and ran out of the back door along the side of my brownstone until I got back to the front. That's when I saw that it was her in the hallway standing outside of my door.

"Kalani, what the fuck are you doing beating on my muthafucking door like you're crazy?" She rushed down the stairs and into my arms.

"I told Tristian about what you and I did and he kicked me out of the house. I'm so lost. I don't know what to do," she cried with tears all over her pretty face.

"What the fuck did you do that for? I thought we was gon' keep that shit between me and you." I tucked my pistols into my pants and led her outside and around to the back door where I came from. I didn't have my keys on me, so I was forced to go back the way I came.

She didn't answer my question until we were safe inside of my house and I'd given her a bottle of apple juice. I'd never seen her look more distraught. Even though her mascara was running down her cheeks, she still looked like a pure dime. That girl was cold as a model and straight out of Brooklyn.

"He's been fronting on me ever since that lil' girl got hit up. I think he fucking around with her mother or something because ever since that lil' girl got hit up, Tristian has been real distant and disrespectful toward me and it's not like him. I don't understand what's going on in his head, but now he's saying he want us to take a break from each other."

"Shorty, I get all of that, but what made you tell him about us? How did I come into the conversation?" She stepped away from me with her head lowered. "He's been acting so fucking soft lately. I brought that up and asked him why he couldn't be more of a thug like you. We talked about a whole bunch of other stuff and then he flat out asked me if I've ever had a thing for you or if we've ever gotten down before. I admitted we did, but I was angry. I wanted to make him feel like shit. The same way he's been making me feel for the last couple of weeks." She pulled out my dining room chair and sat in it.

I took the two pistols off of my waist and set them on the table right next to her. I turned her chair so she was facing me and knelt in front of her. "So you come running to me because of what? You think I'm finna be your savior or something? Huh?" I placed my hands on her thick thighs and squeezed them a little bit. She had on these real tight Nine West jeans that conformed with her body as if they were a second skin. Her thighs looked nice and thick inside of them, bigger than usual. She shrugged her shoulders.

"I wasn't expecting you to do anything in general. I mean your brother had been acting real soft lately, shitting on me. I just wanted to be in the presence of a real thorough bred type of nigga. You already know how I was raised out in the Red Hook Houses. I have been around savages my whole life. I kind of miss that. That's all." She sucked on her bottom lip and looked so fucking adorable to me. Both of her dimples appeared on her cheeks. "You're making me feel like I made the wrong decision or something. I thought I was like your little sister." She avoided eye contact with me.

I squeezed her thick thighs and ran my hands up and down them. "You are. I wasn't saying that you wasn't. I'm just trying to find out what's going on inside of your brain." I forced her thighs apart just enough for me to see her pussy print inside of her jeans. Her lips pressed up against the denim to make their presence known. I could smell her perfume and it was doing something to me.

"Well, can I chill with you for the day or at least until you get up and about? I just need to be around family right now. My head ain't right. It hasn't been ever since he's been treating me like he has.

My dick was throbbing in my pants. She was so thick but small up top though. The more I rubbed up and down her thighs, the more aroused I became. I leaned my face into her gap and pressed my nose up against her jeans, before sniffing loudly. I could smell just a hint of her natural essence. It made me shake.

"Stop, boy. What are you doing?" she asked, trying to close her thighs. "I said I thought I was like your little sister, not your woman."

I kissed the crotch and forced her thighs all the way apart. I stood up and grabbed her hand. "Since the cat is out of the bag, we might as well do us. Ain't no since in you ducking this dick now. What's good?" I pulled her to me and wrapped my arms around her so I could cuff her ass. It was so round in them jeans like a big ass apple. I held the cheeks up and releases them. They fell out of my grasp and jiggled before I cuffed them again.

"Dang, Showbiz. What are you saying? Are you saying you're trying to get down right now?" she asked, still sucking on her juicy bottom lip.

I ran my hand all the way under her plump ass cheeks until I was feeling on her crotch. It was nice and hot. I imagined her panties being wet under the jeans.

"Hell yeah. You know that nigga can't fuck like me. I know what you project girls need. That's why you over here right now. Ain't it?" I sucked on her neck and picked her up, sitting her on top of my dining room table.

"Uh! N'all, that ain't why I came over here, Showbiz. I just wanted to see a familiar face. I'm hurting right now."

I unbuttoned her pants and pulled them down her thick thighs with difficulty. It was as if they didn't want to come off at first, but with some tugging, they made their way down her thighs and off of her ankles. I opened her legs wide and moved her purple bikini panties to the side so I could see her fat pussy lips. They were fully engorged with her clit sticking out of the top of them. I spread the lips.

"I know what you need lil' sis. Trust me, I got you." I sucked her clit into my mouth and ran my tongue in circles all around it. She bucked forward and scrunched her face. "Uh! Showbiz, what are you doing?" She bucked again and caused the table to shake.

"I wanna eat this pussy. Then I'ma fuck it until you start crying. After I'm done, you ain't gon' give a fuck how my brother treating you cause you know I got you." I ran my tongue up and down her wet clit, before sucking on her pearl again. She leaned all the way back and closed her eyes.

"I need you emotionally. I need you to just hold me. It's not just about sex for me. I'm a female. Uh shit!"

She placed the bottom of her feet on to the table and bussed her pussy wide open. I sucked up and down her thighs. I knew what she'd said was the truth. That when it came to healing, women were more emotional creatures where as us men were physical. But I didn't have the patience for all of that shit. I wanted some of that pussy.

It was all that mattered to me. Ever since I'd known her, even from when we were shorties, I'd always wanted to fuck her. I'd only gotten the chance to do it once when my brother was out of town on Spring Break, and even then, I'd had to take the pussy from her sort of. My tongue dove in and out of her, separating her juicy lips. Her essence oozed out of her pink hole and I slurped it up loud and boisterously.

"Showbiz! Showbiz! Aw, damn! I ain't come here for this. Shit!" Her hips rose from the table to bring her mound to my face. I motor boated her sex lips and licked in between them, before nipping at her big clit. I continued to swallow as much as I could every time something ran out of her.

"Szz! Szz! Aw, Showbiz! You got me! You got me! Aww, shit!" She closed her eyes and screamed at the top of her lungs, before shaking like crazy on the table. I sucked on her clit so hard, it was like I was trying to pull it out of her. After she started to cum, I eased up because I knew how sensitive it had become. She hopped off of the table and undid my pants, sliding them down to my ankles. She stroked my dick up and down, running it over her brown cheeks.

"I got you too, Showbiz. You got me and I got you. Huh, let me handle this business."

She pulled back the skin on my stalk and sucked my head into her mouth. Twirling her tongue around it again and again. She sucked all the way to my balls, gagged, and came back up the repeated the process. I grabbed a handful of her hair and guided her up and down my dick. Her jaw hollowed in and out.

She'd pop my dick out of her mouth loudly, licking all over the head while looking me in the eyes. Then she put me back into her mouth and started to suck me at full speed, while she pumped her fist up and down, squeezing it tightly.

I humped in her mouth and rubbed all over her head. That shit felt so good. It was doing something to me just knowing I was letting my brother's bitch suck my dick before I fucked her. I guess I was a dirty nigga at heart, but I didn't give a fuck. I was what I was. This bitch was bad and I had to have her. I needed to buss in her mouth first. It would be my way of claiming a piece of her ass. After all, I'd just eaten her cum. Fair exchange was never robbery.

I sped up the pace and held the back of her head, fucking as fast as I could. She gagged and a bunch of spit dripped out of her mouth and off of my dick. "Suck me, ma. Suck me. I'm finna cum. I'm finna cum. I'm finna cum in yo' pretty ass mouth. Aww, shit!" I groaned pumping my hips into her face. I felt the euphoric feeling of my semen shooting out of my balls and up through my piece before splashing into her mouth. I let some of it fly, then pulled it out and came all over her pretty face. It looked like little streaks of watery ass mayonnaise.

She closed her eyes and tried to turn her head, but I held it steady. "Stop, Showbiz. You so fucking nasty!" she hollered. I pumped my shit up and down until I was done. He still stood nice and tall, fully engorged.

"I want some of that pussy now. I want that shit from the back."

I tossed her a bunch of paper towels. She stood up with her panties still pulled to the side. Her bald sex lips were protruding from her middle, leaking her fluids. I wondered if me cumming in her face had turned her on even more. I knew she liked them thuggish niggas and I was most definitely that. I didn't give a fuck that she was as fine as she was. She felt like she was the shit, but I knew I was.

"N'all, Showbiz. We came, now can we just chill for a minute? I need you to hold me. My head is fucked up."

I grabbed her and bent her over the chair, yanking her panties down her thighs. She yelped and it excited me even more. "Yeah, I got you lil' sis, but first I gotta get me some of this box. I ain't gon' be able to think straight until I do. Open them legs for me." I rubbed her wet pussy. It dripped all over my left hand. She spread her thighs and arched her back, looking over her shoulder at me.

"I hate you for this, Showbiz. Damn, you always gotta get what you want." She reached between her thighs and guided me through the gates of her brown, naked sex lips. As soon as that heat kissed my dick head, I slammed him home.

"Aw! Shit! Beat it up, Showbiz! Don't let me regret this shit." I grabbed her hips and pulled her body forward, then slammed it back into me. Her ass cheeks crashed into my lap, wobbling like crazy.

"I'm finna kill this shit, bitch. I know what you need." I got to long stroking that pussy from the back. Loud slouching sounds resonated from between her legs along with the sounds of our skins slapping into each other's.

*Bam! Bam! Bam! Bam! Bam!. Bam! Bam! Bam!*

"Showbiz! Yes. Yes. Yes. Aww, fuck! Showbiz! Kill it. Kill it. Fuck me harder, Showbiz!" she pleaded.

I smacked her on the ass as hard as I could, while I pumped into her. Her pussy queefed as juices eased out of her. I squeezed her thick ass cheeks and slid my thumb into her asshole.

"Aww, what are you doing?" She smashed back into me over and over, pulling her shirt above her breasts. They bounced back and forth. The nipples were fully engorged.

"Tell big bruh you love this dick! Tell me!"

*Bam!. Bam! Bam! Bam! Bam! Bam! Bam! Bam!*

"I love it! I love it! Aw, shit! I love it, big bro! Fuck me!" she moaned loudly, crashing back into me, creating a loud collision.

*Bam! Bam! Bam!*

I got more and more rough with that pussy. It started to get wetter and wetter. More hot and steaming. The scent from her kitty rose into the air and straight up my nose. Her ass cheeks vibrated every time I crashed into them. There was nothing like fucking a thick ass bitch. It made the pussy feel so much better if you asked me.

She looked back at me and ran her tongue all over her lips, twerking in my lap. "Hit this shit! Hit it harder, Showbiz!" She laid her face on the table and moaned with her eyes closed. "We so bogus! Aw, we so bogus."

I continued to work that ass. I liked watching my dick go in and out of her lips. Her pink inside would come partly out, then go back into her womb. That fascinated me, my gold-colored dick beating down her caramel-colored pussy. Before it was all said and done, I wound up cumming in her four times and she came all over my dick three.

\*\*\*

I hopped off of Kalani's ass and we got into the shower. She washed my body from head to toe and I returned the favor. The whole time I was washing her down, I took my time as I ran my hands all over her sexy temple. I couldn't believe a woman could be so fucking gorgeous and not have a lot of imperfections. I mean she had stretch marks in certain areas like her ass and hips, and even on the back of her knees, but those weren't imperfections to me. Those were things that defined her as a real woman.

I liked them. It made her that much more sexy. Before I finished wiping her down, I ran my tongue all inside of her back door and sucked on her ass cheeks. When you were as thick and strapped as she was, I felt that a man needed to appreciate every facet of that body and I did. We wound up lying in the bed with me on my back and her head on my chest.

"A'ight, lil sis. Now you can tell me whatever you want to. I'm all ears." I laid my big hand on her left naked ass cheek.

" Showbiz, I don't want you to get mad at me, but if I was a man, I'd whoop your brother's ass and kill that bitch and that lil' girl. After all we've been through, I feel like he's putting them before me and that ain't right. Am I bogus for thinking like that?" She looked up at me.

"N'all, you just got a lot of love for him and you're feeling betrayed. It's a natural emotion. Especially since he's trying to kick you to the curb and shit. That ain't right."

"I just don't get it. Ever since high school, he's been encouraging me to be this great woman. I thought it was to complement him as his wife, but come to find out, he don't see any future with me. His mind and heart is already somewhere else. That hurts. It hurts me so badly." She snuggled her face into my chest. I could hear her whimpering. After we got out of the shower, I ducked off and shot a gram into my system, so I was lifted again.

"Yo, fuck him, ma. That nigga gon' do what he wanna do and you gotta do the same. You shouldn't allow yourself to be so weak over another person because when you do, you allow them to take control over you the way that he has. Don't nobody deserve that much credit." I yawned and tried to keep from nodding out. It wasn't that what we were talking about bored me. I was just high as fuck.

"But you don't understand, Showbiz. I have loved that man ever since I was fourteen years old. He's all I've ever known. I didn't have a father around when I was growing up. So the only love I've ever received from any male was from your brother. I didn't even think I was capable of being loved by a man until he came along. Does that sound crazy?"

I shook my head and nodded out. My chin fell to my chest. "Showbiz! Showbiz! Wake up!" Kalani yelled and smacked me on the chest just enough to rouse me. I jerked up just a tad.

"N'all, ma. That don't sound crazy. You grew up in the projects. It's the life we live. I get where you coming from, but you got me now. You ain't got no more worries. Word up." I sniffed loudly and pulled my nose.

"Why do you keep on dosing off on me? Are you tired or what I'm talking about just not interesting enough? You can be honest with me. I'm a big girl."

"N'all, shorty. It ain't got shit to do with what you're talking about. I'm high as hell right now. I shot some of that boy before I climbed in the bed with you. That's all."

"Oh. I didn't even know you did that. I know your brother toot those percocets and stuff. I guess all of y'all get down, huh?"

I smiled. "It's rough out here in these streets. Muhafuckas be needing an escape. You know how it is."

"Yeah, I know I need one right now. How does it make you feel? Does it take the pain away? Both mentally and physically?" she asked, sitting up and placing her hand on my chest. I nodded out. My eyes rolled into the back of my head. A bit of drool slid out of the corner of my mouth on the right side.

"Showbiz, damn. Can you wait to fall asleep? Answer me."

"Yeah, shorty. It take both of them away. I started fucking wit' it real tough after my son and Eve died. It's the only thing that helps me to cope. I been good ever since."

"I wanna try some. I mean not a lot, but at least a little bit until I can get over, Tristian. Can you give me some?"

"N'all, ma. You ain't strong enough to be fucking wit no heroin. Try them lil' pills first and see where that get you. This dog food is for savages only."

"Give me some, Showbiz. Come on. I'll even pay for it. And don't tell me that you don't want to be the one to give it to me, because if you don't, then I'ma leave here and go find me some on my own. I need an escape. You've been through a lot. If you're coping, then so will I."

I don't know what made me jump out of the bed and snatch up my platter of Vega Heroin that I had hidden in the back of my china cabinet, but I did. I brought it back to the bed and sat it on my lap. "Come here, man. Put your hair in a ponytail." I pulled my nose and ran my tongue across my gums. Kalani stood up naked, placed her hair in a ponytail, and sat beside me on the bed.

"It look like cocaine. I tried that one time and I didn't like it. It made me feel too hyper. I like to be calm and mellow like you." I separated the heroin into four lines and picked up the red straw that I used when I used to toot the drug. I handed it to her.

"Look, take it easy. Just clear half a line with this nostril and do the same with this one over here. That way you're balanced out. This shit gon' go straight to your brain. As soon as you feel it, lean back into my chest and let me hold you until I know you're good to go. You hear me, lil' sis?" She nodded and licked her lips.

"I got you." She took the straw and put it inside of her left nostril, tooted half of the thin line, and started coughing. I smacked her on the back.

"You're good. I got you. Now hurry up and hit the other side before you're thrown off. Come on." She coughed a few more times, leaned down and tooted the rest of the heroin with her other nostril. As soon as she cleared the line, she fell back against my chest with a huge smile on her face. Her eyes were low and glossy.

"That shit feel good, don't it? Tell me how you're feel, lil' sis?" She rocked her head from side to side real slow. "I can't feel anything. All I hear is music and I want to laugh even though I know I'm not suppose to be happy." Her eyes were real low. She placed one of her legs over mine and rubbed the side of her face against my chest.

"Now I'm horney all over again. I think I need some more of that dick, Showbiz. Then we need to come up with a plan. We gotta get rid of that bitch and her kid. I'm not gon' be able to cope until I know that whole party over there is broken up."

"I tell you what," I said, sliding my hand down her collarbone and cupping her right breast. "Why don't you turn around and hop on this dick for about thirty minutes, then when we get off, we'll come up with something that will work for the both of us. How does that sound?" She turned around and straddled my waist, reaching under herself for my dick.

"I'm feening. It sounds like a plan to me.

# Chapter 11

Veeto hit my phone early the next morning, waking me out of my sleep. I was laid up with, Kalani, my dick still lodged deep inside of her. We were lying on our sides spooning. I reached over her body and grabbed my phone off of my night table. "What's good, Blood?"

The sun shined through the mini blinds that were on my bedroom window, causing our shadows to cast across the walls. Somehow, I'd forgotten to turn on the air conditioner. I was sweaty and the room smelled like heavy fucking. Kalani had traces of sweat all over her brow.

"Sometimes a muhfucka gotta go ahead and make shit happen for the ones they love, kid. Word is bond," Veeto chimed.

"What the fuck you talking about, son?" I yawned and stretched my arms over my head.

"Got that lil' wet package for you. I need you to pick it up right away though. The whole Harlem watching. Nigga what you gon' do?" he asked. I stood straight up.

"Yo, you got that right now, Dunn?"

"Right the fuck now. Holler at me at my spot in the Bronx. I'll see you when you get here. I got yo' hittas outside to lead the way. One Blood, kid." The phone disconnected.

Kalani kicked her legs in the bed, then opened her eyes. She scrunched her face and grabbed her head. "I got a splitting headache, Showbiz. Something ain't right. I feel like I'm about to throw up." She threw the covers off of her and hunched over. I grabbed the platter of heroin off of the dresser and sat beside her. "You ain't gon' throw up, ma. You're just sick. Here, you need a lil' more of this and you'll be good." I separated two lines and handed her the straw.

She took it. "You're sure? I mean ain't it to early to be doing this stuff? Aw, shit. I gotta get to class." She stood up with the platter in her hand, then doubled over. "Aww, fuck. There's a sharp pain in my side, Showbiz." She made her way back to the bed and sat beside me.

"Look, Kalani. You gotta hit that nose and get this shit back in your system. It's the only way all of your worries will stay as far away from you as possible. Here, now do like I say."

I took the straw from her and held it to her nose. I needed a female partner that I could do that dope with. I missed Eve, and even though I knew that Kalani could never be Eve, at the very least, she could get high with me. Then we could fuck like Jack Rabbits. I mean I would have considered it withTori, but she was already pregnant. I couldn't have her fucking around like that. Doing heroin alone was cool, but it took things to the next level when you had a female companion.

She lowered her head. "Okay, Showbiz. I'm trusting you." She snorted the line hard and held her nose, waited for a few seconds. Then treated the other nostril the same way, before falling back on the bed with her eyes closed and thighs slightly parted. A smile spread across her face.

"You feel a whole lot better, don't you?" I asked, rubbing her thigh.

"Hell yeah, I do. Thank you, Showbiz. I knew you'd hold me down. I'm just gon' lay here for a minute, then I gotta get to school."

"Yo, I gotta go and make a run. I'll be back in a few hours or so. You're more than welcome to chill here until I get back. If you're planning on going to class, then you gotta leave when I leave so I can lock my shit up. What you gon' do?"

"Long as I can use that laptop you got right there, I can handle my school business online. I don't feel like going no where today. I just wanna chill. So I'll be here when you get back. I need some more of that pipe anyway." She licked her lips. I sucked her right nipple into my mouth and pulled on it.

"Alright then. I'll fuck wit 'you in a minute. Keep my doors locked and don't answer them bitches for nobody. You're more than welcome to fuck wit' that raw, just be careful." She sat all the way up and wrapped her arms around my neck, kissing my lips.

"I should have been fucking with you a long time ago. You're a fucking boss, Showbiz. That's hot." She sucked my lips into her mouth and squeezed my dick. "Hurry on back so I can get right."

\*\*\*

When I got to Veeto's crib out in the Bronx, he met me outside where he sat on his stoop with ten Blood killers posted all around him. I pulled up and he hopped off of the stoop. He came to my passenger's window, tapping on it. I rolled the window down. "What it do, Blood?"

"Yo, I got that nigga, his bitch, and their kids zip tied in the studio down stairs. You need to make a mockery of this fuck nigga. Like I said before, the whole Harlem is watching and you already know that Harlem is the epic center of New York when it comes to this drug shit. Muhfuckas know what it is. They know that he knocked off Showbiz, Vega. Now you gotta let them know that that shit can't ride. I got plans for you, kid. You can start your own revolution. I'll stand behind you one hundred percent, me and my thousand plus Bloody Gorillas. Let's roll inside and make this shit happen."

I nodded and jumped out of my whip with murder on my mind. I didn't like this nigga making it seem like I needed him in order to catch and fuck over Wetto. I was my own man. I didn't need no other nigga to validate me or my gangsta. I was Showbiz muthafucking Vega! Soon to be King of the Vegas. If Veeto didn't watch himself, I was coming for his muthafucking slot.

When I got downstairs to the portion of the building Veeto had turned into a makeshift studio, I saw Wetto, his baby's mother, and their two daughters. They were tied to a chair with zip ties around their wrists and ankles along with rope. Me and Veeto stepped into the booth, while the rest of the Bloods gathered around the glass outside of the studio. Not only was Wetto and his family bound to chairs, each of them had black hoods over their heads that looked like pillow cases.

I snatched Wetto's tape off so hard. He slowly opened his eyes, and when he saw me, they got big. He started to murmur into his duct tape. I rolled up the sleeves on my fatigue hoodie, before cocking my right hand back and slapping him across the face as hard as I could. I almost fell over from slapping him so hard. He hollered into the tape as blood poured out of his nose.

"Bitch ass nigga, you had the nerve to fuck over me when I was feeding yo' goofy ass and all of yo' niggas. Where the fuck is yo' loyalty?" I hollered and punched him right in the mouth. He fell backward in his chair, still bound. Veeto rushed over and picked him up.

I stripped the tape off of his mouth. " Nigga explain yourself!"

"Yo, just leave my family out of this shit. I ain't never came at your people on some lethal shit. Them all my little girls, man. I don't give a fuck what you do to me, just leave my babies alone."

*Smack! Bam!*

I smacked the shit out of him across the face, then punched him straight in the nose, breaking his shit. The nose bone turned sharply to the left and his eyes puffed out, turning blue.

"You ain't got the space to save nobody's life, nigga. You about to watch me kill every member of your family right in front of yo' punk ass. I don't give a fuck what you or nobody else thinks about." I stepped to my right and pulled the black hood off of his ten-year old daughter and grabbed her by the throat. She screamed into her duct tape and wiggled as best she could in her chair.

"Yo, come on, Showbiz. Not my kid, man. What happened was between me and you. It ain't have shit to do with our kids. Let them walk and you can torture me for all I care." He struggled against his binds with a mug on his face.

I scoffed and looked into the crying face of his daughter. Her eyes were red. Her hair curly and wavy and looked as if she'd just gotten it done. She shook her head from side to side as if she was begging me to have mercy on her.

"Little girl, what's about to happen to you is all your daddy's fault. He crossed me and because he has, you're forced to pay the consequences with him alongside of your mother and other sister. No hard feelings, okay?" I pulled off the black hoods of his baby's mother and other daughter. All of them were crying. "Everybody, pay attention." I bit into my bottom lip and brought my fist forward into the little girl's face over and over again.

*Wham! Wham! Wham! Wham1 Wham!.*

I could feel my knuckles crushing into her facial bones. I could feel them crack and cave in as my knuckles continued to pound into her again and again. "You. See. What. The. Fuck. You. Made. Me. Do. Weeto? Huh? Nigga?" I hollered, punching her harder and harder. Blood began to pop around my fist. Her eyes rolled into the back of her head as the sockets were shattered. I kept on punching into soft tissue, no longer feeling any bone.

"Alright, muthafucka! Alright! Stop! She's just a little girl!" Wetto hollered, going crazy to try and break his bind with no success. "Stop, you son of a bitch!" he hollered in Spanish.

I continued to punch and beat her head in senseless until she was bleeding out of the sockets of her eyes and nose. I wanted to cause him as much pain as I could. I knew watching somebody kill your child in front of you was the ultimate pain that a man could endure. Especially with the child being a little girl. That had to suck. I could only imagine.

I took a step back and kicked her straight in the chest, knocking her backward to the floor. Before grabbing the hair of her twin, I pulled out my pistol and placed it on safety. Then turned it upside down. "One down, one more to go, fuck nigga. This what you asked for. This what happens to any nigga who cross Showbiz Vega! Any muthafucka. It's Harlem, son!" I raised the gun over my head.

"Please, Showbiz. Look, man. I'll pay you to spare their lives. I'll give you my whole stash. Just let them walk, Dunn!" Wetto shouted with sweat and blood dripping from his face. I lowered my gun and looked over my shoulder at him. "How much are we talking?" The numbers better be all the way up."

"Six mill in cash, fifty kilos of heroin. You can have it all and still take my life. Just let my people live, Blood. It's all I ask. My dying wish." He sniffed loudly.

I turned all the way around to face him. "Oh yeah, that's yo' dying wish, kid? Well, where is all of this treasure that you speak of?" I stood in front of him, ready to slam the handle of my banger up against his forehead.

"My crib out in Staten Island. You can send one of your goons to retrieve it and everything. That shit ain't gon' do me no good if I'm dead, is it?" He looked over at his baby mother, and I noted his face softened. He looked sick.

"Yo,' Blackie. Come here, Son."

Blackie made his way through the doors of the studio. "What it do, kid?" He gave me a half hug and shook up wit' me.

"Yo, this bitch nigga say he got six million dollars in cash and fifty kilos of my shit stashed in his tip out in Staten Island. I need you to take that trip. Snatch that work for me and when you get back, I'll make sure I take care of you just like before. Take two of the homeys you trust wit' you."

I didn't know if I really trusted Blackie as much as I was making it seem, but I had to have somebody go snatch up that package. I was itching to kill Weeto's ass. I mean way more thirsty than I had ever been to kill somebody before in my life.

"Yo, I got you, son. I'll handle this shit ASAP and report back to you as soon as that's a touchdown."

"A'ight, son. Give money all the info that he need so he can make that happen," I ordered Wetto, kicking his inner ankle.

Blackie held out his phone while Weeto gave him all of the info he needed in order to snatch up everything. When he got it all, he grabbed two of the other Blood niggas and they left out the back of the brownstone on a focused mission.

"So you gon' let them go, Showbiz? I mean, son. Can you give me your word that you gon' let my baby mother and daughter go? You've already taken one of their lives. We should be even because I never touched a hair on your people's head and I never would have. These woman and kids ain't got nothing to do with the shit we're beefing over. They're innocent."

I sat back in my chair and smiled at him. Looked at the clock on my phone. Blackie had been gon' for a little over an hour. I'd give him about two before I looked forward to him getting at me. "Nigga, once you hit me, you took food out of my family's mouth. You had the nerve to bumrush my bitch and rub all against her in her shop and shit. Forced her to do yo' bitches hair for no charge. Aw, nigga you brought families into this shit. That's why this lil' bitch laying on the floor dead. Look at her, bleeding all profusely and shit. Sad, ain't it." I curled my lip at him and looked up at Veeto. "Fuck wrong wit this nigga, Blood?" Veeto shrugged his shoulders.

"You know how niggas get when the heat is on. They try and get a muhfucka to see all kinds of logic that ain't there instead of taking that shit like a man. Typical fuck niggas. Nah' mean?"

Wetto sucked his teeth and mugged Veeto. "Nigga, long as I been in the game, I ain't never heard about you putting no work in for yourself. You the type that hide behind monsters because you afraid of the dark fuck nigga. I ain't never did shit to you, so for you to send your hittas at me on this nigga's behalf is blowing my mind right now. I sent some of the dope I took from him to you. So you ain't clean in all of this. It ain't a clean hand in this room."

Veeto stood up and scrunched his face. "Bitch nigga, I told the homey as soon as I found out the lil' business I gave you in regards to his heroin. I ain't know you snuck him for it at first, but once I got wind of it, he was the first number I called. Don't try and use that divide and conquer strategy, my nigga. That shit ain't gon' work.

129

And since you ain't never seen me get down before, how does this work out for you?" He pulled an Army knife out of the holster inside his Marc Jacob Coat pocket, walked behind Wetto's daughter, and pulled her head backwards, slicing her throat from one ear unto the next. Blood skeeted across the booth's carpet. He threw her forward. She landed on the carpet right by my feet with plasma leaking out of her rapidly.

Weeto threw up into his lap. "You sick muthafuckas! I'ma kill both of you niggas one day!" His baby mother was screaming into her duct tape. Tears ran down her cheeks, snot dripping out of her nose. She was shaking like crazy. Her face red like a stop sign. Veeto stepped over the little girl and took his seat, wiping his knife on Wetto's baby mother's face. "Take that shit. Now I put some work in."

# Chapter 12

Blackie dropped the four duffle bags full of money in front of me. "Here you go, Blood. I got the dope outside in the van. You want me to bring that in, too?" he asked, checking the bottom of his Jordans that were saturated in Weeto's daughter's blood. I shook my head.

"N'all, Blood. Half of them yours anyway along with this bag right here. Make sure you hit the Bloods that you took with you. If you eating, then yo' dogs should be eating, too. Word up."

Veeto handed me the bolt cutters. "Yo, y'all pick this botch bitch nigga up and lay him out on that table. Hurry up so we can clean up the mess we're about to make." He stepped back so the Bloods could set Weeto up. They laid him flat on his back along the wooden table in the booth they'd brought in. Once he was sprawled out, they held him down.

"Yo, Veeto. Let me see that knife, kid. I'm about to fuck this nigga over in a major way." He tossed the knife to me and pulled out a bag of Lays Potato chips.

"Do yo thing, Money. Word is bond. I wanna hear that nigga scream. It's soundproof in this bitch, so it's all good." He sat in his chair, but I pulled it up close to the table along with the rest of the Bloods that surrounded it. I jumped on top of Wetto and straddled him like a broad. Took his shirt and cut down the middle of it, ripping the rest of the cloth from his body. He was a real fat ass nigga, sweating and everything. He had *Blood Gang* tatted around his stomach.

"Son, I don't give a fuck what you about to do to me, Showbiz, but when it's all said and done, let my baby mother go. I've held up more than my end of things. She ain't—Aw!" I pressed the point of the knife into the bottom of his Adam's apple and sliced downward, opening and splitting his skin that bled right away. I trailed the blade all the way down to the bottom of his stomach.

He tried to kick his legs and arms, but the Bloods held him down. "Arrgh! Arrgh! You son of a bitch! Why are you doing me like this?" he spat.

I drug the blade backward, using the same incision. The second time caused the meat to tear and open up all the way up. "Yo, hand me them bolt cutters now, son. I got a trick for this fuck nigga since he think he got so much heart."

"Don't do this shit, Blood. You got all of my money. Kilt two of my daughters. I'm still Blood. Y'all can't do me like this. Argh, fuck! Fuck!" he hollered, before his eyes rolled into the back of his head.

I took the bolt cutters, placed it right below his rib cage in the middle where it connected everything. Hook the cutters up to his bone, before closing it together. It snapped as the steel cut through his bone. He began to shake like crazy as if he were having a seizure. Blood ran from his mouth. He gargled on it as his eyes remained in the back of his head.

I didn't give no fucks. I went to one rib at a time, cutting them with the big tool. One after the other until his entire rib cage folded inward. I grabbed my pistol and beat on his chest with the handle caving it all the way in. It looked like he was imploding. Veeto handed me his knife again. "Yo, you a crazy ass nigga, Showbiz. Muhfuckas gon' know what it is when it comes to you, kid. Word is bond. New York on notice."

I slammed the knife into Weeto's chest and sliced downward, digging into his flesh. As soon as the hole was big enough, I stuck my gloved hand inside of it, feeling around for his heart. His eyes fluttered. He hopped up and down on the table, choking. Blood poured out of his nose, mouth, and ears. I grabbed his heart, and with all of my strength, I pulled it as hard as I could until it came out of his body with the arteries attached to it. I yanked until the heart popped off of them. I held his heart, his bleeding heart in the air.

"This what happens to anybody that crosses Showbiz Vega! Spread the word. And kill that bitch. No mercy style!" I snapped. I felt like I was losing my mind. All I saw was red. I had a blood lust. My vision was hazy as the blood dripped from my gloves and my forearm. My chest heaved up and down and I couldn't see straight.

\*\*\*

As if that wasn't crazy enough, my father summoned me and my brothers to his pad later that night. I got there at around ten o'clock. I was fucked up, high as hell. Still seeing the images of Wetto and his slain family in my mind's eye. I took my seat at the table and closed my eyes. I was still having problems with my vision. My brother, Miguel, sat next to me, texting away on his phone while Tristian sat directly across from me with an amused look on his face. He looked like he'd just gotten done fucking or something.

"Yo, kid. Why you got that dumb ass look on your face?" I asked before closing my eyes back. The air conditioner in the room was on full blast. It was fucking with my high because I could feel the goose bumps appear all over my skin. It was freaking me out.

"You gon' see in a minute, god. Yo, just honor me, and fall back, too."

Minutes later, my father came into the room and cleared his throat. "It's good to see all of you. I won't make this meeting too long because I know that time is money. I would like to formally announce my successor. I ask that everyone respects my decision because a deal is a deal. I said the first son to come to me with fifteen million dollars would be able to take my seat after I stepped down. Well, Tristian has done that and therefore, he will be my successor. Son, come up here."

Before Tristian could even rise from his seat. I stood up. "What the fuck are you talking about? I know damn well he ain't came up with no fifteen million dollars. This is some bullshit. It's foul play involved!" I snapped ready to make my way to the front of the room.

"Juanito, have a seat. I am speaking right now," my father retorted. I could see his face turning red.

"N'all, fuck that, Pop. You've always been all up this nigga's ass anyway. Deep down in your heart you want him to be your successor, it didn't matter if either me or Miguel came up with everything anyway." I mugged my father with mounting hatred.

"Juanito, I'm not going to tell you again. If you don't—" He grabbed his heart. "Argh!" He fell backward toward his wheelchair and missed it, landing on the floor.

I bucked my eyes. "That's what you get. That's karma. Karma always comes back to get a nigga. That's my muthafucking birthright! Mine! You can't take that away from me!" Tristian fell to the ground with him, along with my uncle Javier. My father held his chest as his face turned blue. His mouth was wide open with his tongue laid against his cheek.

"Come on, Pops. Please don't die. Don't die, Pop," Tristian cried. I didn't give a fuck. I hated his guts. I was hoping he died right there on the floor. He was worthless to me. Had God not taken him, I would have. I hated him that much. I would make Tristian pay for stealing my birthright. I would make him pay in the worst way. There was no way around it.

My father began to seize, shaking like crazy, before he was as still as a board. His tongue hung out of his mouth. I stepped by them. "Come on, Miguel. This ain't got shit to do wit' us. I didn't give a fuck about Miguel either, but I had a trick up my sleeve. I couldn't allow for Tristian to keep breath in his lungs. Not holding on to my birthright. He had to pay. That thief of a bitch nigga had to get what was coming to him and I was going to use Miguel to handle that business for me. I was thinking of killing two birds with one stone.

\*\*\*

When I got back to my crib, I found Kalani laid out on the bed, butt naked with her legs wide open. She trailed her fingers through her gap and sucked on her bottom lip. "I been missing you like crazy, Showbiz. I don't know why, but my pussy is purring like crazy." She pulled them out of her gap and stuck them into her mouth. "What's wrong with you?"

I dropped the duffle bags on the floor. "My old man just died, but before he did he gave my brother the rights to his throne. I can't let that shit ride." I moved my dresser out of the way,so I could get to my safe. I needed to stuff them as much as possible before I drove out to my mother's crib and filled my safes up that were there.

"Your dad died. I'm so sorry to hear that, Showbiz. Are you okay?" I shrugged my shoulders.

"It is what it is. I ain't gon' shed no tears over that shit. Life goes on. Nah' mean? Oh, that nigga Miguel in the front room, so you might wanna throw some clothes on before he makes his way back here. I know you ain't trying to be on display like that." I started to load my safe. She stood up and slid her panties up her thick thighs and then her jeans. Her titties bounced on her chest as she fit her bra in place.

"Do you want me to leave, Showbiz? If he see me back here, what is he gon' say to Tristian?" she asked, buttoning her blouse.

"I don't give a fuck what he say. That nigga Tristian don't hold no governance over me. We fucking, it is what it is. You acting like you're afraid of that nigga. If that's the case, you can get the fuck out. Word up."

She shook her head. "Baby, you don't have to be so mean. I'm good where I'm at. I was just thinking of you and his relationship. I know that whatever takes place with me, it doesn't matter because you guys are still blood. But forget I even said anything."

"Bitch, go get in the shower. Then come out here and clean this room up. I got some chicken in the refrigerator that I want you to cook, along with some white rice and pinto beans. Handle that for me. I'll appreciate it. You hear me?" She unbuttoned her blouse and dropped her jeans, walking toward the bathroom with her panties all in her booty.

"Yeah, I heard you and I got you. Let me hit this water first. Do you mind if I wear one of your long button ups when I'm out?"

I shook my head. "N'all, just make sure you stay away from my Ferragamo and we good."

Miguel tapped on the door of my bedroom. "Blood, what's good. You got me out here like a outcast waiting for yo' ass. What's on your mental, kid? My baby mother just got wind that my Pops died and she's freaking out. They were close," he hollered through the wooden door.

"Yo, I'll be out in a minute. Just wait for me in the living room while I'm putting this shit away."

"A'ight, son. I'm giving you ten minutes, then I'm back in my whip and headed to Queens. I'ma grab a pop out of this refrigerator, too. I'm thirsty as a muthafucka."

I was irritated and felt like snapping on his ass but instead, I bit my tongue and finished loading my safe. Ten minutes later, we were sitting in the living room watching Lebron's debut with the Los Angeles

Lakers. He tooted a thick line of Vega's heroin and sat back.

"I wanna smoke that nigga, B. I ain't gon' even lie. You know him and me ain't never got along and never will. You know it had to be some dirty politics involved. Tristian ain't even in the streets like that. Where the fuck he get fifteen million from?" he asked, pulling on his nose.

"Not only that, but Pops said that in addition to the fifteen million, that we had to take over the Red Hook Housing Projects. That fool ain't did that. I got my hittas out scouring the city right now looking for Wisin and Chulo. As soon as either one of them are located, they gon' hit my phone. In order to take over the Red Hook Houses, we gotta go through them. Them niggas ain't no pushovers. And Tristian ain't about that life. Trust me, kid." I looked up to the screen and watched LeBron cock back and dunk on a nigga from Golden State. I wished that he'd landed in New York. It was time for us to see another NBA title.

"Yo, I see you got Kalani in the back. I been wanting to fuck her black ass since I was like nine. I don't really like Black bitches, but I'll fight through my disgust to fuck that bitch."

One of the reasons I ain't like Miguel being around me was because he was one of those racist Spanish muthafuckas that always had something slick to say about Blacks in general. Even though we were the same complexion as the caramel ones. If you didn't hear us speaking Spanish, you would have never guessed we were anything other than Black.

"Yo, don't worry about what me and shorty got going on. Stay in yo' lane before I buss yo' brain, nigga. Word up. And you know I don't like all that racist shit around me, so keep that shit to yourself." I mugged him and looked back toward the television screen.

"My bad, bruh. You know I ain't mean nothin by it. But I get your drift. Anyway, why did you want me to follow you back here?"

"Because you gon' smoke that nigga, Tristian and then I'ma give you a slot under me. I'ma start my own chapter of Bloods and of our family. Put the both together and label us Vega Bloods. I want to bring up some of our family from Havana too after we take over the Red Hook Houses. But before any of that can occur, you gotta smoke, Tristian. The mission will bring you a hundred gees. Since your girl pregnant and all, I figure you gon' need that money. Am I right?"

I picked up my bottle of Moet and turned it up. In my opinion, Miguel wasn't nothing but a send off. Just like Tristian, he ain't have no real heart. Neither one of those niggas was meant to be king. I hated both of them and as far as I was concerned, the only blood I had was my mother. I had some love for Tori, but it wasn't enough to cement her in my heart.

" o, for a hunnit gees, son, I'll smoke him and whoever else you need me to hit. I'm hurting right now. I got like twenty gees in the bank and that ain't shit. You already know it's finna get hectic real fast for me."

"Then it's settled then. We gon' hit that nigga after we put pops in the ground. It might be smart to put his body right on top of the old mans since Pops was always kissing his ass anyway." I couldn't help laughing at my own joke. Miguel tooted a line of heroin and nodded.

"Sound like a plan to me. Yo, you bringing Tori to our old man's funeral? I was thinking about bringing Ariana, but I ain't sure."

"Nigga, neither me or any of my bitches is gon' be at that dead nigga's funeral. Let Tristian fill it up with guests. Fuck him. I said what I said before his heart stopped beating. No more words are needed. Word is bond. Fuck him." Kalani strolled out of the kitchen and stood in the doorway of the living room.

"Showbiz, your food is done. Is there any thing in specific that you'd like to drink so I can have it ready for you?" she asked, looking like a sexy ass Goddess.

I shook my head. "N'all, ma. I'ma sip on this Moet and eat my meal. You think you can put another plate together for Miguel.?" She scrunched her face and frowned.

"I sure can't. As many monkeys as he's called me? That punk ass nigga can make his own plate." She rolled her eyes and turned around, walking away as her shirt billowed around her. A glimpse of her purple panties all in the crack of her ass was seen. I couldn't do nothing but shake my head.

"Yo, fuck you then and I stand by what I said about yo' ass in the past, gorilla bitch!" he yelled, standing up. I cringed and jumped up. Before I could think to stop myself, I hit his ass with a right hook and knocked him clean out.

"Nigga I told you about that racist shit. You gon' respect these sistas when you in my presence. Word up. Yo' dumb ass got Black in you, too but you're too stupid to know it.

Kalani ran into the living room with a knife in her hand. When she saw Miguel laid out on the floor she stopped in her tracks.

"Oh damn, baby. You already handled that nigga then, huh?"

"Yo, go make my food and set my shit on the table. Don't ever interrupt me when I got company again or I'ma put my foot up yo' ass. You got that?"

She nodded and blew a kiss at me. "I do and I'm sorry."

## Chapter 13

I loved having my two hit squads because it meant all I had to do was send out an order and wait for it to be carried out. Blackie's squad located Chulo and Wisin a week after my father's funeral. His crew had caught them slipping, fucking with a couple escorts out in Manhattan. By the time he contacted me, they'd already been bound and gagged. He waited for the order to execute, but instead of giving it to him, I had other things in mind. I waited an additional three days before I got in touch with Bruno Gomez. By the time I'd already fucked over Wisin's inner family and hit his ass for ten million dollars, I'd taken Tristian along for the lick to throw him off of my scent and intentions to kill him.

I met up with Bruno Gomez on a Thursday night at Trump Towers. When I stepped into his penthouse suite, the first thing I saw was that every armed bodyguard in his circle was female. They had black masks over their faces and guns in their holsters. Their eyes were low. Their lashes were nice and long. He greeted me with a handshake.

"Juanito Vega, what an honor it is to meet you. I've heard about the decision Chico made to give his throne to his second born instead of his first. That's a pity. Something like that would never happen in the Gomez family. Please have a seat."

The only soldier I had roll out with me was Blackie. After he'd turned over two big scores without dipping into the pots, I felt like I could trust him a little bit. I was ready to give him a slot in the Vega Bloods.

"I hear what you saying Bruno, but the way shit looking right now, if you don't play your cards right, you won't have a son to pass your throne down to."

I grabbed a bottle of Champagne out of the bucket of ice on my way to the leather couch where two of his bodyguards stood behind it with their guns out. Bruno sat across from me and Blackie. He was a sharply dressed man in a tailor made suit. He was clean shaven, had thick, wavy gray and black hair with thick eye brows and golden skin.

"I assume that means you know where my children are? You should also know that I've placed a one million dollar reward on them. If you've called this meeting for the money, just tell me where they are and you can walk away with a million dollars in cash tonight."

I sat back on the leather couch and took a long swallow from the champagne. "Don't insult my intelligence with such a small figure. I know that your children, especially your sons, mean everything to you. Without them, you have no one to leave your dynasty too. I mean we all respect women. Of course you could easily leave the Gomez's throne to one of your little girls, but that wouldn't sit right with you, now would it, Bruno?"

He took a cigar from a box of Cuban cigars and one of the female bodyguards came and lit the tip. He puffed on it a few times until smoke wafted into the air. He inhaled a puff of it, before blowing it to the ceiling. "If you got something on your mind, why don't you say it, Juanito?"

"Not only do I know where both of your children are, but I know whose taken them and for what purpose." He sat on the edge of the couch.

"I'll give you five million for the information right here and right now. Let's not play any more games. You help me get my sons back and you're a rich man."

I smiled. "I'm already rich, Bruno. And once again, you insult my character with such small offers. I'll tell you what, why don't you dismiss your guards to the adjoining room and I'll do the same here to Blackie. When they leave the room then, you and me will be able to talk some serious business. How does that sound?" I grabbed one of the Cuban cigars out of the box and sniffed along the length of it. It reminded me of the ghettos of Havana. I missed them and had not been in a few summers.

Bruno held up his hand. "Listen up, ladies. Take this man right here into the next room so Juanito and I can discuss some serious business. Show Blackie here a good time. Let's go." He clapped his hands together after saying all of that in Spanish. He waited until all of them left the room before he got up pacing back and forth with his right hand in his pocket. "For over thirty years, the Vegas and the Gomezes have been at each other's throats. The war started over fifteen acres of sugar cane land. My grandfather and your great grandfather were given thirty acres of land that were forced to share. Only the soil in fifteen acres of the land was rich enough to produce a steady flow of sugar cane.

Well, you can imagine that two poor, headstrong workers would fight for the rights of the rich soil. So the war has carried on and on over thirty years. When your father Chico and I was old enough to step out into the real world, we left Havana and came to New York where we dove head first into the drug trade. I used a few plugs from Honduras to get my operations up and running right there in the Red Hook Housing Projects.

Chico used Debra's connections in Chicago that had strong ties to the many cartels in Mexico. Both of us were able to generate enough money to purchase more and more of the sugar cane fields out in Cuba until we accrued enough land to present before our families. The sugar industry had fed our families, both yours and mine, for over twenty years until Chico found a way to convert the soil to process the plants that we use to make our heroin and cocaine. He's quite the genius I must admit.

But even with all of his smarts, he's a very stubborn man. This war between the Vegas and Gomezes could of ended a long time ago had he agreed to a sit down where our families. We could have come together to overpower the Castros, but I digress. Let's stay in the moment. " What are you seeking for the safe return of my children? I am willing to go as high as fifty million a piece." He turned around to face me.

I shook my head. "It ain't about the money, Bruno. It's about the partnership. I want to extend to you something that my father never had the commonsense to extend."

Bruno laughed. "What partnership can you possibly render unto me? You're not even moving into Chico's seat. Tristian is, the son of Debra, though I can't really say that was a blind side. He's always

146

had a soft spot for that boy because of his mother. But if I was looking to mend fences between the Gomezes and the Vegas, I would request a sit down between him and I."

"I don't give a fuck about Tristian. I, Juanito Showbiz Vega, am going to be king of the Vegas. Not Tristian! Now it is in your best interest to hear me out, Bruno." My heart was beating fast inside my chest. My vision was going hazy. I was ready to snap the fuck out.

Bruno nodded and held up a hand. "Alright, alright, Juanito. Calm down. Everything is going to be okay. I didn't mean any disrespect by it." He sat across from me and crossed his legs. "Proceed and let me hear you out."

"Tristian, for the time being has taken over my father's throne, and his first order of business is to wipe out the Gomezes which are, as you know, our closest rivals, both here,] and back home in Havana. To start to his rule off on the right foot, he snatched up both of your sons. Being that I am insubordinate to him, I had to go along with it. However, when he was ready to murder them in a bloody fashion, I stopped it. I stopped it because I see this as a opportunity for me to rise up in the ranks of the Vegas and in the underworld where the Vegas and the Gomezes are neck and neck. I am looking to take over the throne and to reclaim my birthright. In doing so, I 'd like for us to be partners on a respectful level."

"That son of a bitch put his filthy hands on my boys. Where the fuck are they? Tell me! Tell me right this instant! I can't take anymore of the suspense."

"Your children are safe and sound, Bruno. I know what you want. Now you need to listen to what I want so we can come to an understanding. You get that?"

He stood up and flared his nostrils. "Well, go ahead, Juanito. What do you want?"

"I need you to help me burn the surface of the Vega's fields. Not the actual crops, but I need it to look that way. You see, my father did a lot of shady business with a Russian by the name of Kosov. Are you familiar with him?

"Putin's nephew. A cold hearted son of a bitch that likes to take advantage of the Spanish. He thinks we're dumb and incapable of maintaining our productive land. He's tried numerous times to buy into the Gomez's fields and I've rejected him every time. Your father was into him for fifty million, but I've heard that Tristian has been settling that debt. Why do you want to burn the fields?"

"I don't want to burn them completely, just the surface. I need for my family and the Russians to think that the fields are destroyed. They will begin to panic and think that they will be forced to starve and go without in a short amount of time. And that's when I will step in as the savior and they will beg me to lead. By this point, I will be looking for the Russians to have moved on to greener pastures. You understand?"

He pulled at the hairs on his chin and nodded his head. "Yeah, I guess I do. But what about Tristian? He has to pay. I can't sit back and know what he's done without making him pay."

"I'll take care of Tristian. There is already a plan in place. If it is not carried out the right way, I'll see to it myself that it is. But since harm was brought to your family, I feel that I owe you an eye for an eye. I will give you full permission to attack and destroy the Vega's mansion and all of the occupants up in it. Murder everybody."

Bruno raised his eyebrow. "What are you looking to gain by this act? Those are suppose to be your loved ones." He sat back on the couch and crossed his legs.

"We gon' start the Vegas from scratch. All of them muthafuckas love my brother more than me. They need to be vanquished. I am the new head and anybody that refuses to fall in line under me or doesn't honor me as king, will meet their bloody end. That's the way it's going to go. After all of these acts are taken care of, you and I will sit down and discuss how we'll work cohesively to conquer the narcotics world of the United States and abroad. Now what you think about that?"

He lowered his head and appeared to be in deep thought. "And you say you're going to kill Tristian? What if I said I wanted that right in order to cement this deal between the two of us?"

He looked up at me and lowered his eyes into slits. If I could find a way to get in good with Bruno Gomez, get my footing into the underworld like never before, then I can orchestrate a plan to oust him and takeover everything that he'd built. Not only would I be filthy rich, but I'd be the most powerful Vega to ever walk the face of the earth. I'd make my father turn over in his grave again and again.

"Like I said before, there already a plan in place. If it botches, then he's all yours. As long as I get to watch." Ever since my father had given him my birthright, I'd hated Tristian's guts with a passion.

"There's one more thing before we shake hands. Your brother, Tristian, and Debra, have opened two warehouses they use strictly to distribute the Vega's heroin and cocaine. Both are in the meat-packaging district. These warehouses are cash cows and protected by Senator turned Mayor Jeffery Grant. If you and I are to come into partnership, I want in on those plants and some of the rights to Mayor Jeffery Grant."

"As long as I'm in the room and included in all deals that have anything to do with him or his leverage, then I am all in. As far as the warehouses go, you help me burn the top layer of the Vega's fields and extinguish it, then we have a deal with those two things. What do you say?"

He smiled. "Juanito Vega, you're a shrewd and cruel businessman, but I think we're going to make a lot of money together and conquer a lot of shit. I can't say that I'm not worried about you because you are so relentless, but all that says is that I'm lying in the bed with the right type of monster.

Now, lets go so I can get my kids back. Oh, and I'll overlook what took place with Wisin's woman. Lucky for you I didn't like her, and the kid wasn't a Gomez. I'll act as if these things never existed. You're welcome." He held out his hand for me to shake. He was speaking about the incident that Tristian and I had done together. We'd snatched up Wisin's woman and kid and I'd murdered them both while in search for ten million dollars of spoils. I didn't give a fuck about their lives and had honestly forgot all about it.

I shook his hand. "It's in the best interest for both families that you have." That night, Wisin and Chulo were returned to Bruno, so our deal was expected to go into place. Even with both Wisin and Chulo swearing their revenge.

## Chapter 14

"My fucking gun jammed, Showbiz. I was bucking his bitch ass down and my gun jammed!" Miguel hollered, standing in front of me with his gun in his hand.

Blackie stood off to the side. "I should have gotten out of the car and made sure he was dead, boss but your strict orders was for me to let him handle his business, so I did. Tristian just might be dead though. There was a lot of blood that splashed against the windshield." He sat back on the couch and pulled a fat blunt from behind his ears, lighting it.

I turned off my big-screened televison and stood up. "Nigga, sit yo' soft ass down and let me think. Damn, I sent you to do one fucking thing and you can't even do that. How fucking hard would it have been to run to the car and get Blackie's pistol so you could finish him off? Huh?"

He sat on the couch and shook his head. "I wasn't thinking, Showbiz, honestly. Once my shit jammed, I just panicked and wanted to get out of there. Then I looked like somebody was peeking from out of his crib. My head was spinning, kid. I mean what would you have done in that position?"

*Smack!*

I open handed his ass as hard as I could. "Muthafucka! Those are a bunch of excuses. I am Showbiz Vega. I sent you a mission, a mission that was supposed to be completed and carried out, but you boffed it. If it would have been me, I would have stayed there until the job was done because that's what killers do! So don't give me that my gun jammed shit!"

"Boss, I can go finish that nigga once we locate what hospital he at if he didn't die. I ain't got no problem handling that light work. I'm trying to get my footing in your crew anyway."

I smiled. "You sound like a fucking killer to me. That's what a killer sound like. They don't make all of these fucking excuses of why they didn't lay a nigga's ass down. They just handle bitness." I mugged Miguel with pure hatred. "I should make you smoke this fuck nigga, Blackie. Word up."

Miguel jumped to his feet. "Wait a minute, Showbiz. I'm still your brother, Dunn. You can't let some other nigga kill me just because I made a mistake. I'm still a human."

"Nigga, I can do whatever the fuck I want. I run this show. Say, Blackie? You wanna smoke this bitch nigga and show him how it's done?" I asked, looking Miguel in the eyes. Blackie stood up and pulled his .44 Desert Eagle from his waist band and placed it against Miguel's temple.

"Blood, all you gotta do is say the word and it's a wrap." He cocked the hammer. Miguel swallowed and closed his eyes. His head was bent at an awkward angle. "Come on, Showbiz, man. I'm your brother, kid. You can't do me like this. I look up to you," he said, whimpering.

I looked him up and down in disgust. "Tsk! You ain't no fucking brother of mine. You're more of a sister. Look at you, trembling like a straight bitch. Nigga, you scared to die? Huh?"

Blackie bit into his bottom lip. "Say the word, boss. I'll splatter his shit all over this living room."

"Don't let him do it, Showbiz. Please, man. I'll find Tristian and finish the job. I promise."

I shook my head once again, "Yo, Blackie stall his soft ass out. He don't want them problems, son." Blackie took the gun away from his temple and placed it on his waist. "Yo, I'll still smoke Tristian. Ain't no sense in you sending junior to do the job. He might fuck it up again. I'll make sure I don't. That's on my Blood, kid."

I turned to Miguel. "Son, from here on out, I don't want to hear you claiming that you're a Vega. Change yo' name, punk or feel the wrath of my hittas. There's a new king of our blood line and you're looking at him. It's best that you get as far away from New York as you can. Next time I cross paths with you, it's gon' be one, son. I'm icing you. Word is bond. Now get the fuck out my tip! Get!"

He rushed towards the door, grabbing the handle and unlocking it. Before he stepped out, he looked over his shoulder at me. "I still love you, Showbiz. I don't give a fuck how you're getting down on me. You're still the one I look up to and I always will. That's on my unborn seed, kid."

I pointed towards the door. "Nigga, get yo' soft ass out of my crib before I give the order to have you smoked. I ain't gon' say that shit again!"

Blackie stood up and took his pistol off of his hip again. He aimed it in Miguel's direction. "Step off, Blood. You heard what the boss said."

Miguel rushed out of the door and slammed it. I could hear his loud footsteps as he traveled down the stairs and out to his car. I wanted that nigga out of my life. In my opinion, he was a black eye to the Vega family. Way too soft and weak. I wanted to purge my bloodline of all of its soft niggas. I wanted to build up an army of monsters like myself. Killers that would protect our bloodline and got to war at all costs. I was on a focused mission to recreate my people.

\*\*\*

Tristian wound up murdering Miguel two weeks later, cutting up his body and throwing it over the George Washington Bridge. I didn't give a fuck he had killed Miguel. I knew that he would be next, and then there would be no dispute over who my father's throne belonged to.

In addition to the death of Miguel, Bruno Gomez held up his end of the deal. He had the Vega's fields set on fire. At the same time they were set on fire, his killers rushed the Vega's mansion in an all out warfare. I hadn't gotten the report of who'd survived or died, and to be honest, I didn't give a fuck. Now that the acts of my plan were going into effect, it was up to me to continue to keep things moving in the way that I needed them too.

\*\*\*

It had been nearly a month since I'd sent Tori away into hiding. She been hitting my phone like crazy every single day since then, and I'd taken my time responding back to her. I was kicking it with

Kalani so tough that I just didn't have the desire to fuck with Tori on an emotional level. I felt I would get to her when I got to her and that would be that.

It was Saturday night, and Kalani and I had been getting fucked up the entire day. I'd shot at least four grams of heroin into my system and watched Kalani toot about two grams. I was so high that I could barely keep my eyes open. My ears were ringing and my dick was so hard that it hurt.

We were sitting in the living room of my crib when Kalani stood up and pulled off her short t-shirt. Underneath, she had on a pair of pink G-string panties. But she had them on backwards so that the string went in between her thick, brown pussy lips. Drake's "In My Feelings" was blaring out my speakers. She placed her hands on her knees and turned around so her ass was facing me. It had gotten fatter since her and I had started to fucking around with each other.

"Showbiz, watch me twerk this big ass booty for you." She started to pop it up and down to the song. *"Showbiz. Do you love me... Say you'll never ever leave from beside me..."* she sang before getting down on all fours and really popping that pussy like crazy. The string split her slit down the middle and rode up and down her crux. I could see her asshole's crinkle, as well.

My dick got even harder. I pulled it out of my hole and stroked it up and down, while I watched her do her thing. The way her ass jiggled, along with her thighs ,got me to beating my meat like crazy. Every time she popped backward, her brown lips would open up to reveal her pink insides. It looked so good to me. She laid her face on the ground and balled her fist, beating it on the carpet while her pussy popped up and down. She was clowning.

"Look at that ass, Showbiz."

She looked over her shoulder at me and ran her tongue all over her lips, before continuing to do her thing. I was so horny by this time, precum was all over my finger. I took my hand off of my dick and got behind her with my face. I forced her body to the carpet, opening her ass and licking in between her cheeks.

She cocked her right leg all the way upward along her rib cage. "I knew you was gon' come get this shit. I knew you couldn't watch yo' baby do her thing without touching her. Uh, shit. Eat me, Showbiz. It's okay," she moaned, holding her ass cheeks open for me.

I sucked on her anus and slid my tongue into it. It was super tight and hot. I kissed her pussy lips and sucked them into my mouth. Then slid my tongue back up to her asshole, worming it inside of her. I wanted to fuck that big ass booty. "Kalani, I'm about to fuck this ass, ma. I gotta have some of it right now." I ran my dick up and down in between her cheeks.

She reached under her stomach, rising up from the ground just a little bit to do so. When her hand got between her legs, she spread her pussy lips wide showing me her hole. "You can do whatever you wanna do, baby. But if you gone fuck my ass, you better long stroke the hell out of it. I need all of that pipe in this big ol' thang." She smacked it loudly.

I ran my dick head in circles around her pussy hole, getting it nice and wet. Her essence was leaking out of her like clear syrup. I coated my helmet with it and brought it up to her asshole, forcing it inside of her. She looked back at me with her face scrunched. "Damn, Showbiz. It feel like your shit is twice as big for some reason." I smacked her hard on the ass. *Smack!*

Watched it jiggle and worked my hips from side to side until my head popped inside of her. Once in, I slammed it home hard.

" Uh!" she groaned as I spread her knees further apart. "Kill that big booty. Take me to Harlem, daddy."

She bounced back into me with her mouth wide open. I gripped that big ass booty. My fingers held the flesh of that ass. It felt like a soft pillow. It was meaty and hotter than a furnace it seemed. Her anus squeezed my shit so tight that it felt like I was being suffocated. I slammed it home deeper and then pulled back, bringing some of her inards with me, before I pushed them back in with my pipe. I built up a nice rhythm and got to tearing that ass up.

*Bam! Bam! Bam!*
*Smack! Smack! Smack!*
*Bam! Bam! Bam! Bam!*

"Uh. Uh. Uh. Shit! Showbiz! Fuck that ass, daddy! Fuck that ass just like that! It's yours!" she hollered and bounced back into me faster and faster, while she played with her clit. She opened her lips wide. Her fluids ran out her and down her thick thighs.

*Smack! Smack! Smack!*

I loved watching that ass jiggle while I hit it from the back. I could smell the scent of her sweat and just a hint of ass and perfume waft up my nose. The smells combined motivated me to go ape shit crazy. I got to stroking her like a monster. She laid her face on the carpet and screamed as I grabbed a handful of her hair. "Aw, shit! Aw, shit! Fuck me, Showbiz! You're killing this ass. Yes!"

*Smack! Smack! Smack!*

"Say it's Harlem, ma." I breathed out of breath. "Say it's Harlem, right now!" I growled, speeding up the pace. My hips crashed into her soft ass and it felt so good.

"It's Brooklyn, nigga. Fuck that!" she screamed. "You. Ain't. Running. Shit. Aw, baby!" She closed her eyes and continued to slam back into me.

"Bitch, what?" I flipped her on to her back and forced her into a ball. Slid my dick back into her open anus that looked like a pink mouth before I slid back into her and got to fucking her like my life depended on it. "Say it's Harlem, bitch! Say it!" I could smell the aroma of shit now. My dick ran in and out of her guts at full speed. She was farting and everything.

"Never! It's. Brooklyn. It's. Fucking. Brooklyn. Mama! Mama! Aw, shit. Mama, make him stop!" she screamed. I bit into her neck hard and started to clench my teeth together, while my hips rose and fell against all of that ass. She was trapped and couldn't move. Couldn't do shit but take all of my dick. And it was doped up and wouldn't go soft for a long time. "Say it, say it."

She continued to play with her clitoris. "Aw, fuck! You're killing me. You're killing me. I'm finna cum. I'm finna cum so hard! Oh! Oh! Oh! It's

Harlem! It's Harlem, mama!" she whimpered and started to shake like crazy.

Just hearing those words got me to shooting my nut all in her ass. I pulled my dick out and bussed all over her stomach in big globs. My chest heaved up and down. Sweat trickled down the side of my face.

# Chapter 15

"Showbiz? Showbiz? Wake yo' punk ass up and tell me why this bitch is laying in my spot," Tori hissed and placed a cold metal object to my forehead. My eyes open and looked into the angry face of Tori. Her eyes were low and menacing. She held a .45 to my head with the hammer already cocked. I passed gas and felt my stomach turn into knots. "Yo, what the fuck are you doing, Goddess?"

"N'all, nigga. You answer my muthafucking question. Y'all got this house smelling like nothing but sex. You got me all the way in Jersey, worried about yo' monkey ass and this is what you're over here doing? You're fucking Tristian's bitch. Nigga, what's really good?" She blinked and tears dropped from her eyes.

"Shorty, if you don't get that fucking gun out of my face, I swear to God I'ma kill yo' stupid ass. You never pull a gun on a nigga unless you're ready to kill him. Real killers don't talk. It's too many words coming out of your mouth for you to be on some killer shit. So check yourself."

I started to sit up. Tori climbed off of me and put the barrel to Kalani's head. I didn't know how she was sleeping through all of this, but she was. She was knocked out. It seemed as if she were in a coma.

"Showbiz, I swear to God if you don't tell me what the fuck is going on, I'ma waste this bitch. Did you know there as a pregnancy test in the bathroom and it's positive?" she asked, wiping tears from her cheeks.

I slid from the bed and stood up. I shrugged my shoulders. "Bitch, fuck what you talking about. I should pop yo' stupid ass for putting that pistol to my head." My stomach was in knots. I felt sweaty and lightheaded. I was feening for my dope. I needed to take a hit and fast. I was jonzing like crazy this morning. Snot slid out of Tori's nose.

"You don't respect me, Showbiz. Ever since you and I have been together, all you've treated me like is shit. Why the fuck am I in Jersey and this bitch is here laying in my spot? Tell me!" she yelled.

Kalani's eyes popped open. When she saw Tori had a gun aimed at her, she tensed up and tried to scoot away from her. "Tori, what the fuck are you doing?" she asked with her eyes bugged out of her head. She was butt naked.

"Bitch, you laying in my nigga's bed and you gon' ask me what the fuck am I doing? I think it's perfectly clear what I'm doing." She pressed the barrel to her forehead and placed a knee on the bed so she could reach her better.

Kalani grabbed her wrist and pulled it away. "Bitch!"

*Boom!*

The gun went off and sent a single slug into the wall, right past my left shoulder. It put a big hole in the wall. I jumped to the side just in the nick of time. Kalani head butted Tori in the face, splitting it. Blood gushed out of her nose and mouth. "Fuck you think this is," Kalani grumbled, still struggling to take ownership of the gun.

Tori grunted. "I'ma kill you, bitch. I'ma kill you. You fucking my man." More blood ran out of her nose and over her lips. Kalani head butted her again, this time so hard, Tori let go of the gun and fell backwards and off the bed. Kalani rushed her and straddled her body. She took her head into her hands and held it, before slamming it into the hardwood floor.

*Bang! Bang! Bang!*

"Bitch, it ain't sweet.

Bang!

"I don't"

*Bang! Bang!*

"Know what you think this is." She started to bang her head into the floor over and over on a rampage.

I stood back and got my works together. I was too sick to intervene. Nothing else mattered more than me getting my fix. I drew the dope up into the syringe and placed it at my forearm's vein, before pushing down on the feeder. The drug rushed into my system and gave me the strength that I was missing. I smacked my lips together and closed my eyes as the girls grunted in their struggles behind me. I opened my eyes in time to see Kalani put the gun to Tori's eye socket.

"I'm tired of bitches taking my kindness for weakness. Tide of you hoes, period!"

*Boom! Boom! Boom!*

She stood up and aimed down at Tori's body.

*Boom! Boom! Boom! Boom!*

The fire spit from the .45 and caused Tori's body to jump from the floor again and again. Blood popped from her body and sprayed the walls. I lowered my head and took a deep breath, before walking over and looking down on her. The heavy smell of gunpowder and blood was in the air. Tori had massive holes in her face with blood gushing out of them. Half of her skull was blown off. Both of her eyes were wide open. Kalani had popped her in the face, head, neck, and chest. She was twisted and there was nothing that I could do about it.

"You saw what that bitch tried to do to me, Showbiz. You saw that she came at me first. I would have never did that shit if that bitch ain't try and kill me first." She looked back down at Tori and shook her head. "Fuck, I'm finna go to jail for the rest of my life. What the fuck was I thinking?"

I took the gun from her hand. "You ain't finna go to no fucking jail, shorty. I'ma take care of this shit. You hear me?" I held her little chin in my hand.

"Yes, I hear you, Showbiz. I ain't mean to smoke yo' bitch, but fuck that. She could have killed me."

I grabbed her by the throat and slammed her against the wall, right where they'd left a big ass hole.

"Bitch, you listen to me. You never have any remorse after you kill something. Fuck that. Remorse is for suckers. You smoked her ass and that's just that. Life goes on. Any muthafucka put a gun to your head is supposed to die. She was starting to look too much like Punkin to me anyway. Come on, help me get this carpet from the other room so we can roll this bitch up in it."

We spent the next fifteen minutes doing exactly that. Once I had her ass rolled up in the carpet, we carried her out back and into Kalani's trunk. Later that night, my mans Blackie helped me chop her ass up and throw her into the river. I didn't give a fuck she was pregnant with my seed. All I saw was the fact that, that bitch had put a gun to my head.

Had Kalani not smoked her, I would have eventually ended up doing it. I lived by the code that if a muthafucka upped a gun on me and didn't pull the trigger, then I would at my earliest convenience. Tori would have been dead a whole lot sooner had I not needed my dope so bad.

\*\*\*

I heard that Tristian had killed the infamous Russian drug lord who went by the name of, Kosov. Bruno had briefed me on the matter. I didn't know what that meant for the family, but I could only assume that Tristian's ass was out. It was rumored that Kosov was a Putin. If that was the case, then that meant that my brother would have the ultimate beef for the rest of his life. I needed to find a way to disassociate the Vega name from that of Tristian. He was in hot water and there was no way our people would have any shelf life standing behind him.

I got in contact with Bruno and asked him to meet me at my Waldorf Astoria suite I'd booked while I was looking for a new place after Tori's murder. I could no longer be in that house without feeling her spirit all around it. It had been three weeks since her murder and even the hot and heavy sex between me and Kalani couldn't shake that eerie feeling of her.

I refused to stay at her crib. I was an independent nigga. Bruno wound up accepting my offer to meet and we met up at twelve midnight the day after I'd requested the meeting. He greeted me with a hand-shake. He had his son Wisin with him.

"Juanito, it's good to see you, son." He shook my hand and held my elbow, then kissed me on both cheeks.

I wiped at my cheeks with my shoulders. "What the fuck? You just getting back from France or something?" I asked, feeling grossed out. I didn't like no fucking man putting his lips on me. I didn't care what custom he was following or trying to duplicate.

"How did you know, son? Can you smell the French whores all over me?" he asked with a smile on his face.

I shook my head. "Hell n'all and I ain't trying to either. I just don't like you kissing my cheeks and shit. Handshaking is enough. Y'all come on in and make yourself comfortable." Wisin stepped into the suite and mugged me with an obvious hatred. He looked up and down with his upper lip curled. "Showbiz."

I laughed. "I can see you still harboring some ill will toward me. Even though I'm the one that saved your life. Ain't that a bitch."

I closed the big door behind them. I had my Vega Blood niggas stationed all around the room. They wore black bandanas with red specks over their faces. So much so that you could barely make out their eyes. They also had black hoodies with red trim pulled over their heads. They looked like deadly ninjas with assault rifles in their hands.

"Saved my life? Nigga, if it wasn't for you, my daughter and my fiancé would be alive right now. Damn my life."

I shook my head. "Nah, son. My brother smoked yo' people. I was in the car, but it was my idea to tie them up and leave them that way. I wore a mask so I wouldn't have to kill them, but he had other plans in mind. To each their own. My job was to keep you and your brother alive. That's what I did. My job is done." Wisin lowered his eyes.

"N'all, kid. You one of those dirty niggas. The streets talk. I heard about how you fucked over Wetto and his whole family. Ain't no way you were a part of that lick on my Band-o and you ain't buss your gun. I know better than that, even if my father don't. I'ma respect him for now, but when the time is right, Juanito Vega, yo' ass is mine. That's on my land. You can mark those words."

I was seconds away from smoking him and his punk ass father. I'd never let a nigga threaten me and live to tell about it. I reached under my shirt for my pistol when Bruno called out to Wisin. "Wisin, sit your ass down and shut the fuck up! What did I tell you, huh?" he shouted in Spanish.

Wisin mugged me and slowly walked past me and his father. "I hear you, Dad. Excuse my behavior." He continued to look into my eyes with a vicious stare.

I smiled. His body language was all the words I needed. I knew I would have to handle his ass. There was no way I could allow him to keep breath in his lungs knowing that he held a deep hatred for me. I took my hand off of my pistol and sat on the couch across from them. "Please, have a drink. I got Hornitos, Patron, and Ciroc." I pushed the liquors closer to them.

Bruno held up a hand. "No, thank you. Let's get down to business. Tell me, Juanito. What do you need from me?"

I popped the cork on the Patron and sipped from the bottle. "I need to know whose going to take Kosov's seat. As you know, Tristian has put him under. I know how this shit goes. When you cut the head off of a snake in the Underworld, the only thing that happens is another one takes its place. I need to know whose taking Kosov's place?"

"That would be his brother, Vorsky. He's a ruthless son of a bitch that has mad billion dollars in the tech world. He's dibbled and dabbled in narcotics from time to time, but most recently, he's been more active. He's looking to buy heroin-producing land. There's been a demand for the drug in the United States. Its stocks are up by forty percent.

I am sure he'll be looking to capitalize on the projects that his brother, Kosoc, have left behind. He'll also be looking to avenge his death I'm sure. That spells trouble for the Vegas and anybody aligned with them. I hope you know that."

I laughed. "Fuck all of that. How do we reach out to him? Do you have his contact information, and if so, can you get me a sit down like ASAP?" I sat the bottle of Patron back on the table and sat back with my arm along the back of the couch.

"I guess I will take a drink." Bruno grabbed a glass from the table and poured himself a double shot of Hornitos, swallowing it down in four big gulps. He set the glass on the table.

"Sounds to me like you're worried about the Russians, Juanito. If you are, you should be. They're a deadly bunch of low life muthfuckas with no regard for mankind. They've been looking for a reason to steal more of the land in Havana, and what Tristian has done has given them a green light." He sat back. "I can get you a sit down, Showbiz, but I don't know how useful it's going to be under the circumstances. They don't like our people. And we don't like theirs.

Not only are their politics involved, but there is a battle for supremacy in the drug world. The Russians not only want to rule and run America, but they have a deep hatred for us Latinos. It reports all the way back to Fidel Castro and Guatemala. Someday, I'll sit you down and break it down for you bit by bit. But for now, we have to get Vorsky's ear. It's extremely imperative that we do so. It's the only way we will be able to flourish and our treaty will remain intact."

I sat on the edge of the couch. "If you get me that sit down, Bruno, I will be very grateful and will extend my sincerest gratitude to you. I may not be in a powerful position just yet, but I assure you I will be very soon."

Bruno stood up and extended his hand. "Juanito, I'm going to hold you to it." We shook hands.

I looked over his shoulders and into the eyes of Wisin. I didn't give a fuck what took place with me and his father. That nigga was a dead man walking. I had visions of making him suffer before I took him from the face of this earth.

*\*\*\**

That night, I held Kalani in my arms on some lovey dovey type shit. I don't know why I was feeling so sappy, but I just needed to hold her. We laid in the big bed with the pool about twenty feet away from us. She laid on her side and rubbed all over my chest. I was high as fuck as I tried to put everything into perspective. I could feel her hot thigh draped across my waist, her pussy on my hip scorching me. Ever since I'd watched her murder Tori, I'd started to take a liking to her more than I wanted to admit.

The lights were dimmed. The sounds of SZA resonated from the speakers that were placed in the corners of the room. There was a nice reflection on the ceiling coming off of the pool. There was a scent of chlorine and perfume in the air. She rubbed me down to my stomach.

"Baby, do you remember when Tori said there was a pregnancy test in the bathroom and it was positive?" She looked up at me and into my eyes.

I gripped her ass and held it. "Yeah, I remember. What about it?" I knew what she was getting at and I wasn't for it.

"Well, of course it was mine. And, of course, I'm pretty sure you've figured out that I'm pregnant. I'm not that far along, but I still want to know what you want to do about it?"

I laughed and frowned. "Shorty, you been fucking with that raw for almost two months now. You can't bring no baby in the world and you doing that shit. That shorty won't stand a chance."

"But what if I stop doing that dope right now? Do you think you might be up for us having a baby together?" I slid my hand in between her legs and opened her pussy lips with two fingers.

"On some real shit, I ain't ready for no kids. I got too much going on. I could leave this earth any day now, then what would my shorty have? Huh?"

I rubbed my fingers together. They were sticky with her juices. That was one thing I could say about Kalani. She had some good ass pussy. It was hard for me to kick her to the curb. Every time I thought I was getting tired of her, my dick twitched. She had me pussy whipped, but not the kind that would stop me from going up side her head if she stepped out of line. I was still Showbiz. Wasn't no bitches pussy gon' change that.

"I figured you'd say something like that, Showbiz. Damn. That leaves me with a dilemma." She sat up and my fingers fell out of her seeping hole. I sucked them into my mouth, smacking loudly on the digits. She tasted slightly salty, but sweet at the same damn time.

"Yo, don't get to acting some time of way and shit. I'm just keeping it one hunnit wit' you. I don't see no kids in our future right now, but I do see us being together. I find myself kind of hooked on yo' lil' strapped ass. Don't let that shit go to yo' head because I'll still fuck you up, but I like having you around. Plus, with all of that knowledge in your head, we're going to need it. I look forward to buying up as much real estate as I can. Owning property is long lasting wealth and riches."

"I kind of want to have this baby though, Showbiz. I mean, we could clean up our acts, right? If it came down to it and I really got to handling my business in the corporate world, would you be willing to go all the way legit?"

"One hundred percent, without a shadow of a doubt, hell muthafucking n'all! I don't give a fuck what you do. I got my own agenda and a kid ain't part of the equation. I ain't trying to have a baby until I'm in my late thirties and got at least two hundred million in the bank. My sole focus right now is restoring my last name. Now I want you along for the ride, so you're free to come, but if you keep hollering this baby shit, I'ma have to replace you. It is what it is. What you gon' do?"

She exhaled loudly and wiped her nose with the back of her hand. She dropped her head and shook it. Her lips were moving, mumbling to herself. I figured she was trying to talk herself into going with what I put down.

"Yo, what you gon' do, lil' one. You starting to irritate me."

She shrugged her shoulders and gave me a look of defeat. "I'm trying to be apart of you for a long time, Showbiz. This decision isn't easy to make, but I mean if you're not trying to go there with me, then I guess it would be pretty ignorant for me to try and raise a child on my own. My mother did that and even though she did the best she could, we struggled a whole lot. So, just come with me and we'll take care of this situation together." She got up and walked toward the bathroom that was connected to my bedroom. Before going inside of the door, she turned around to face me. "I wasn't even sure if it was yours or Tristian's anyway, so I guess it's for the best. I'll set up the appointment."

"Yeah, do that and I'll make sure I'm wit' you, ma. I'm sorry shit ain't work out like you planned, but it'll be plenty of time for us to have a shorty down the line. Right now, let's focus on getting our bank right. The goal is two hundred million for me. I ain't gon' sleep soundly until I stash that. Word."

T.J. Edwards

# Chapter 16

When I stepped into Vorsky's office on Wall Street with Bruno Gomez just a little bit behind me, I couldn't believe my eyes at what I saw. First of all, the office was very spacious and clean. It had all sorts of paintings by Leonardo Davinci all over the walls. His desk had a pink laptop and a pink box of Kleenex. Vorsky met us at the door with a handshake that was less than firm. He had jet-black, wavy hair, shaved on the sides. Big blue eyes with makeup on to cover up his blemishes I guessed. He was sharply dressed in a Burberry business suit with matching loafers.

In his right arm was a little white dog that was the size of a poodle. The dog also had on a Burberry outfit and it's paws were covered with Burberry doggie shoes. I was taken back because I was expecting some vicious Russian thug with a scowl across his face. Instead, I was met by this cheerful person with very little bass in his voice.

"You must be Juanito Vega?" he asked, shaking my hand. I noticed that his nails were manicured and covered with clear polish.

"The one and only. It's a pleasure to meet you, Vorsky. We have a lot to talk about."

He walked behind his desk and sat his dog in his lap, rubbing its fur. "Not really. Your brother killed my older brother. Somebody needs to pay for that. You need to tell me how you are going to convince me not to have every living Vega massacred." He lowered his eyes, and looked over to Bruno." Oh, where are my manners? It's good to see you, Bruno. You look like you've gained a little weight."

Bruno shrugged his shoulders. "I've been doing a lot of traveling and haven't had a lot of time to hit the gym. Hey, but what are you gonna do, am I right?"

I was sitting there in my chair fuming. I couldn't believe the introduction of this bitch ass Russian. I felt like he'd just threatened my whole bloodline. "Damn that fucking Tristian." I thought out loud.

"Well, Juanito? I'm waiting?" Vorsky asked, crossing his legs. I sucked my teeth and looked into his eyes. There was mascara around them. "What are you looking for?"

"I find it hard to believe that Bruno hasn't clued you in on my interests." He looked over at Bruno. "I am looking for land. Land is greater than money. You have five hundred acres. I want half or we go to war. Half and the life of your brother."

"You want two hundred and fifty acres of our Vega's land. Are you fucking kidding me?" I asked, feeling my heart pounding in my chest. Looking across at this muthafucka, I couldn't see no threat in him at all. He looked more feminine than masculine. I felt like giving him two to the dome right then and there, but Bruno and I had checked our guns in at the door.

Vorsky smiled and continued to pet his dog. "Well, excuse me, Juanito, but we are in New York. You must always start the bid high, but I am open to listening to your counter. Go ahead darling, wow me." He batted his eyes and smiled brightly.

"Yo, don't be calling me no fucking darling. I got respect for you, Vorsky. Let's keep this shit on a name by name basis, none of that pet shit. Nah mean?"

"Oh, I see that somebody is a little homophobic. Sure, we'll see things your way. Go ahead and present me with your proposal. I'm all ears, Juanito."

I was trying to keep calm. I felt like this muthafucka was mocking me or something. And it wasn't that I was homophobic I just wasn't cool with a man calling me no fucking darling. Shit, I'd never been with a female that called me that, so it was weird. Nevertheless, I wasn't about to have this dude calling me anything but my name. Point blank period.

"I'm not willing to give any of my family's land. But what I can do is give you a life for a life and twenty five million dollars for the inconvenience. I didn't have shit to do with your brother being killed, but I'm willing to compensate you anyway just so we can squash this bullshit."

"Unfortunately, you're not offering me anything that I want other than your brother's life. A piece of your land had to be apart of the equation or we go to war. It's as simple as that and please do not let the soft spoken demeanor fool you. If we go to war you will lose in a bloody fashion and so will your innocent loved ones. This will be the biggest mistake that the Vega' have ever made. It is in your best interest to play ball with me. This I can assure you of." He smiled and placed a tuft of hair behind his ear.

The last thing I wanted was to go to war with this Russian. Bruno already told me how powerful he really was. I was still in the beginning stages of building up my army of savages. There was no way I was ready to go to war with a billionaire mad man who probably had something to prove to the rest of the underworld because of what had taken place with his brother.

I had to put my ego to the side and use my brain. And my brain told me that losing some of the land was better than losing it all. There was a season for everything and this wasn't the time nor the season for me to pick a fight with a nation of real killers.

"Fifty acres of land. You do with it what you please, but your men don't overstep that fiftieth acre of land barrier."

"One hundred acres and you take the life of your brother. I want you personally to bring me his head on a platter and present it before me. There is always room for a little sibling rivalry. Wouldn't you say, Juanito? In exchange for this display, I will not only wipe the slate between you Vegas and us Putins clean, but I will also help you take your family's business global. There's only but so much money in the United States. You have to start to think euros and yens. Pretty soon, the American dollar will be worth the same as a peso. Trump is a idiot." I exhaled through my nostrils.

"Yo, you reaching for a hundred? How about we make it seventy five and I give you ten million."

"I've said what I'll accept. Anything less than this is a lost to me. You can either shake on this deal or we can make further arrangements."

He picked his dog up and allowed for it to lick his lips. He kissed the dog in the mouth and I'd had all that I could take. I couldn't believe I was about to be hoed by a person that kissed his dog in the mouth and spoke softer than a woman. I was heated and wanted to kill something.

I extended my hand. "We got a deal, Vorsky. Long as you hold up your end, I'll do the same."

He shook my hand with a limp wrist. "That is very wise of you. I would like your brother executed first thing in the morning. I'd like to have his head on a platter right here on my desk by tomorrow afternoon around lunch time. Make it happen."

\*\*\*

I stayed up the whole night with my back against the bathroom door, shooting heroin. I had was so fucking mad when I got home, I didn't know what to do. I couldn't go at the Russian directly because he'd have me vanquished. I was sure of that. Tristian was surrounded by old world bodyguards from Havana, so it was going to be a task going at his ass. I had a bunch of things to figure out before the morning and the only way I knew how to free my mind was by the help of Mrs. Heroin.

So I got fucked up all night until I passed out on the floor of the bathroom with the syringe laying on the floor right next to me. Before my eyes closed, I'd came up with the perfect plan of attack. I would make sure that Tristian's head was placed before Vorsky just as he'd requested. Only then could I move forward with my life and get things on track.

\*\*\*

"Showbiz! Showbiz! Baby, what the fuck is going on? Are you okay in there?" Kalani asked, beating on the door. "Showbiz!" I jerked in my sleep and opened my eyes in a frenzy. My head was pounding worst than ever. I rushed to the toilet and purged my empty guts inside of it, retching like crazy.

"I'm good, baby! I'm just sick." I felt like I was on fire. Like I had on three sweaters, even though I was shirtless. Sweat was all over me.

"Baby, I think I fucked up. I need you to come out here or I'm about to lose my mind!" Kalani hollered. "Please!" I flushed the toilet and gargled some Scope, spitting it into the sink and running the water. I washed my face with a towel and opened the door. Kalani stood on the other side of it with her eyes wide, tears running down her cheeks. She had blood all over her Prada blouse.

"Baby, I got her. I got the lil' bitch. Now I wanna kill her. I need you to stop me from killing her baby, please." She held a long serrated knife in her left hand. There was blood dripping from the blade.

My inner forearm was itching like crazy. My bones felt like they were cracking and my head was pounding. I needed a fix. I couldn't fully focus on what she was talking about until I got right. I brushed past her and dropped to my knees, sticking my hand under the hotel mattress in search of my product and found none. There should have been at least an ounce of Vega heroin there. I was about to flip out.

"Kalani, where is my dope, baby? I'm sick. Where the fuck is my shit?"

"Baby. I got a little girl in the conjoining room. I've already started working on her. I swear I don't want to kill this little girl. You have to stop me." Sweat poured from her face in rivers. Her eyes were glossy. Her hair was all over the place. She was shaking like crazy. I could tell that she was beyond high.

"Kalani, what little girl are you talking about? And where is my shit? It ain't under the bed? I'm sick, baby." My stomach muscles tightened up on me. I hunched over, looking up at her. She ran and opened the door that led to the other room that was connected to ours.

"Brittany! The little girl that got shot the same time your son and Maine did. She took Tristian away from me. It's her fault. I'm gon' finish killing this bitch, bae." She ran into the other room and straddled the little girl with the knife in her hand. From the distance, I could see that Brittany's mouth was duct taped.

"Where the fuck is my dope, Kalani?" I felt all under the bed until my fingers came upon the plastic wrapper the dope had been in. I pulled it out and saw there was nothing left inside of the bag other than a few crumbs. I sucked my finger and the saliva on my digits helped the crumbs to stick to my finger. I stuck it up my nose and snorted as hard as I could, searching for some relief from my withdrawals, but receiving none.

"Bitch, you did all my dope. I'm finna kill yo ass!" I snapped, struggling to get to my feet. I dry heaved and fell to my knees. I crawled across the floor. My vision was blurry. My hearing distorted. I felt like I needed to shit and throw up at the same time.

"I'm finna kill this lil' bitch, bae! I'm so sorry. It's her fault! It's her fault, daddy!" Kalani hollered from the other room.

My phone began to buzz from the dresser top. There was a pounding at the door. I felt like my heart was about to burst. I couldn't breathe. I squeezed my eyelids tight and took a deep breath. I crawled to my phone and read the face. There was a text from Blackie, saying they were ready to handle business and all of our troops were in place.

Kalani stepped back into the room with blood all over her. It dripped off of the knife. "I'm so sorry, Showbiz. I can't take this shit no more. I can't let you do me like this." She raised the knife over her head and rushed at me with an ear-piercing scream.

To Be Continued...
King of New York 5
Coming Soon

## Submission Guideline

Submit the first three chapters of your completed manuscript to ldpsubmissions@gmail.com, subject line: Your book's title. The manuscript must be in a .doc file and sent as an attachment. Document should be in Times New Roman, double spaced and in size 12 font. Also, provide your synopsis and full contact information. If sending multiple submissions, they must each be in a separate email.

Have a story but no way to send it electronically? You can still submit to LDP/Ca$h Presents. Send in the first three chapters, written or typed, of your completed manuscript to:

**LDP: Submissions Dept**
**Po Box 870494**
**Mesquite, Tx 75187**

*DO NOT send original manuscript. Must be a duplicate.*

Provide your synopsis and a cover letter containing your full contact information.

Thanks for considering LDP and Ca$h Presents.

**<u>Coming Soon from Lock Down Publications/Ca$h Presents</u>**

BOW DOWN TO MY GANGSTA

By **Ca$h**

TORN BETWEEN TWO

By **Coffee**

BLOOD STAINS OF A SHOTTA **III**

By **Jamaica**

STEADY MOBBIN **III**

By **Marcellus Allen**

BLOOD OF A BOSS **V**

By **Askari**

LOYAL TO THE GAME **IV**

LIFE OF SIN II

By **T.J. & Jelissa**

A DOPEBOY'S PRAYER **II**

By **Eddie "Wolf" Lee**

IF LOVING YOU IS WRONG… **III**

LOVE ME EVEN WHEN IT HURTS **III**

By **Jelissa**

TRUE SAVAGE **VII**

By **Chris Green**

BLAST FOR ME **III**

A BRONX TALE III

DUFFLE BAG CARTEL III

By **Ghost**

ADDICTIED TO THE DRAMA **III**

By **Jamila Mathis**

LIPSTICK KILLAH **III**

Mimi

WHAT BAD BITCHES DO **III**

A HUSTLER'S DECEIT 3

KILL ZONE **II**

BAE BELONGS TO ME III

By **Aryanna**

THE COST OF LOYALTY **III**

By **Kweli**

SHE FELL IN LOVE WITH A REAL ONE **II**

By **Tamara Butler**

RENEGADE BOYS **III**

By **Meesha**

CORRUPTED BY A GANGSTA **IV**

By **Destiny Skai**

A GANGSTER'S CODE **III**

By **J-Blunt**

KING OF NEW YORK V

RISE TO POWER III

By **T.J. Edwards**

GORILLAZ IN THE BAY III

**De'Kari**

THE STREETS ARE CALLING II

**Duquie Wilson**

KINGPIN KILLAZ IV

STREET KINGS 2

**Hood Rich**

STEADY MOBBIN' **III**

**Marcellus Allen**

SINS OF A HUSTLA II

**ASAD**

TRIGGADALE II

**Elijah R. Freeman**

MARRIED TO A BOSS II

**By Destiny Skai & Chris Green**

KINGS OF THE GAME II

**Playa Ray**


<u>Available Now</u>

<u>RESTRAINING ORDER **I & II**</u>

By **CA$H & Coffee**

<u>LOVE KNOWS NO BOUNDARIES **I II & III**</u>

By **Coffee**

<u>RAISED AS A GOON I, II, III & IV</u>

<u>BRED BY THE SLUMS I, II, III</u>

<u>BLAST FOR ME I & II</u>

<u>ROTTEN TO THE CORE I III</u>

<u>A BRONX TALE I, II</u>

<u>DUFFEL BAG CARTEL I II</u>

By **Ghost**

<u>LAY IT DOWN **I & II**</u>

<u>LAST OF A DYING BREED</u>

BLOOD STAINS OF A SHOTTA I & II

By **Jamaica**

LOYAL TO THE GAME

LOYAL TO THE GAME II

LOYAL TO THE GAME III

LIFE OF SIN

By **TJ & Jelissa**

BLOODY COMMAS I & II

SKI MASK CARTEL I  II & III

KING OF NEW YORK I II,III IV

RISE TO POWER I II

By **T.J. Edwards**

IF LOVING HIM IS WRONG…I & II

LOVE ME EVEN WHEN IT HURTS I II

By **Jelissa**

WHEN THE STREETS CLAP BACK I & II III

By **Jibril Williams**

A DISTINGUISHED THUG STOLE MY HEART I II & III

LOVE SHOULDN'T HURT I II III

RENEGADE BOYS I & II

By **Meesha**

A GANGSTER'S CODE I &, II III

**By J-Blunt**

PUSH IT TO THE LIMIT

By **Bre' Hayes**

BLOOD OF A BOSS **I, II, III & IV**

By **Askari**

# T.J. Edwards

THE STREETS BLEED MURDER **I, II & III**

THE HEART OF A GANGSTA I II& III

By **Jerry Jackson**

CUM FOR ME

CUM FOR ME 2

CUM FOR ME 3

CUM FOR ME 4

An **LDP Erotica Collaboration**

BRIDE OF A HUSTLA **I  II & II**

THE FETTI GIRLS **I, II& III**

CORRUPTED BY A GANGSTA I, II & III

By **Destiny Skai**

WHEN A GOOD GIRL GOES BAD

By **Adrienne**

THE COST OF LOYALTY

**By Kweli**

A GANGSTER'S REVENGE **I II III & IV**

THE BOSS MAN'S DAUGHTERS

THE BOSS MAN'S DAUGHTERS II

THE BOSSMAN'S DAUGHTERS III

THE BOSSMAN'S DAUGHTERS IV

THE BOSS MAN'S DAUGHTERS **V**

A SAVAGE LOVE  **I & II**

BAE BELONGS TO ME I II

A HUSTLER'S DECEIT I, II, III

WHAT BAD BITCHES DO I, II

By **Aryanna**

190

A KINGPIN'S AMBITON
A KINGPIN'S AMBITION **II**
I MURDER FOR THE DOUGH
By **Ambitious**
TRUE SAVAGE
TRUE SAVAGE II
TRUE SAVAGE **III**
TRUE SAVAGE **IV**
TRUE SAVAGE **V**
TRUE SAVAGE **VI**
By **Chris Green**
A DOPEBOY'S PRAYER
By **Eddie "Wolf" Lee**
THE KING CARTEL **I, II & III**
By **Frank Gresham**
THESE NIGGAS AIN'T LOYAL **I, II & III**
By **Nikki Tee**
GANGSTA SHYT **I II &III**
By **CATO**
THE ULTIMATE BETRAYAL
By **Phoenix**
BOSS'N UP **I , II & III**
By **Royal Nicole**
I LOVE YOU TO DEATH
**By Destiny J**
I RIDE FOR MY HITTA
I STILL RIDE FOR MY HITTA

By **Misty Holt**
LOVE & CHASIN' PAPER
By **Qay Crockett**
TO DIE IN VAIN
**SINS OF A HUSTLA**
By **ASAD**
BROOKLYN HUSTLAZ
By **Boogsy Morina**
BROOKLYN ON LOCK I & II
By **Sonovia**
GANGSTA CITY
By **Teddy Duke**
A DRUG KING AND HIS DIAMOND I & II III
A DOPEMAN'S RICHES
HER MAN, MINE'S TOO I, II
CASH MONEY HO'S
**By Nicole Goosby**
TRAPHOUSE KING **I II & III**
KINGPIN KILLAZ I II III
STREET KINGS
By **Hood Rich**
LIPSTICK KILLAH **I, II**
CRIME OF PASSION I & II
By **Mimi**
STEADY MOBBN' **I, II**
By **Marcellus Allen**
WHO SHOT YA **I, II**

**Renta**

GORILLAZ IN THE BAY **I II**

**DE'KARI**

TRIGGADALE

**Elijah R. Freeman**

GOD BLESS THE TRAPPERS I, II, III

THESE SCANDALOUS STREETS I, II, III

FEAR MY GANGSTA I, II, III

THESE STREETS DON'T LOVE NOBODY I, II

BURY ME A G I, II, III, IV, V

A GANGSTA'S EMPIRE I, II, III

**Tranay Adams**

THE STREETS ARE CALLING

**Duquie Wilson**

MARRIED TO A BOSS…

**By Destiny Skai & Chris Green**

KINGS OF THE GAME II

**Playa Ray**

## <u>BOOKS BY LDP'S CEO, CA$H</u>

<u>TRUST IN NO MAN</u>

<u>TRUST IN NO MAN 2</u>

<u>TRUST IN NO MAN 3</u>

<u>BONDED BY BLOOD</u>

<u>SHORTY GOT A THUG</u>

<u>THUGS CRY</u>

<u>THUGS CRY 2</u>

<u>THUGS CRY 3</u>

<u>TRUST NO BITCH</u>

<u>TRUST NO BITCH 2</u>

<u>TRUST NO BITCH 3</u>

<u>TIL MY CASKET DROPS</u>

<u>RESTRAINING ORDER</u>

<u>RESTRAINING ORDER 2</u>

<u>IN LOVE WITH A CONVICT</u>

**<u>Coming Soon</u>**

BONDED BY BLOOD 2

BOW DOWN TO MY GANGSTA